COURAGE OF THE TRAVELER

MORE BOOKS BY TONI BINNS

Nexus Universe - Traveler Series

- Traveler Forgotten (*Short Story*) - Available at tonibinns.com
- Choice of the Traveler
- Call of the Traveler
- Courage of the Traveler

Nexus Universe - Seer's Fate Series

- Visions of Blood and Feathers

Nexus Universe - MEOW: Magical Emporium of Wares

- Serial available at meow.tonibinns.com

COURAGE OF THE TRAVELER

TRAVELER
BOOK THREE

TONI BINNS

BARDHWOOD PRESS, LLC

"Courage is not the absence of fear, but rather the assessment that something else is more important than fear."
Franklin D. Roosevelt

CHAPTER
ONE

B right, white light glittered over the room, coming from a large oval stone set in the center of the floor. The room was huge, with floors sloping slightly downward toward that glowing stone. The great wooden beams of the high ceiling drew likewise together at the room's center.

This stone was clearly important, and not only because it glowed—it called to Betha. But she resisted, staying next to the elder by the doorway.

"It is the Sky Stone, given to us by the Starwalkers." The elder Talli's voice was soft as a line of gargoyles trailed out of the room. Each was hurt, some wounds visible, others wrapped in bandages. "It was the sacred trust we broke. It was entrusted to us, and in return, we gave our oath as a people to do our part. A few generations ago, a charismatic leader asked why we should keep serving this trust. He said it would be easier, and better for our people, to let the injured and those who lost the sky deal with their curse on their own. Too many listened, too few spoke in support of the trust, and we had not seen a Starwalker for many generations. And so it was that the room was blocked off..."

A gargoyle approached the glowing stone, one wing gone. A smaller gargoyle helped him walk across the stone floor. They paused before the stone, and the smaller gargoyle stepped back. Silence reigned in the area as the injured one reached out. His hand hovered above the stone, mere inches away, and Betha held her breath.

Whispers were barely beyond her hearing. Like someone was just too far away to make out the words, but you knew they were saying something. Then his hand landed on the stone. Light flickered then washed over the room before receding, like a wave at the shore.

Betha gasped. His wing was whole, and he was standing tall. The gargoyle next to him jumped up in his arms. She felt the joy in the moment, even from the distant doorway.

"This room stayed blocked off until Magson tore down the barricade with his own hands. His pain was so great, no one could stop him. Though after many years, this place had been almost forgotten, so not many tried."

"This is what you mean by the trials?" Betha motioned around with her hands to the line. She had thought the trials were something like a competition or a quest. Not touching a stone. How could you fail?

Talli nodded. "The stone decides if you are worthy to be healed, but it is a bargain. You are given the sky back, but eventually, you hear the call. It leads you to a portal to bind with."

"Is everyone healed, then?" Betha studied the round, white stone and the next gargoyle that walked forward. His arm was in a sling, and he limped with pain, eyes focused on the white stone. He didn't hesitate before placing his hand down. The light flared, and he smiled proudly.

"No, Starwalker. Not everyone is healed. Sometimes they vanish into the stone. Many vanished in the first week of us opening the room. Less now."

Betha turned away from the stone, though everything inside her screamed to touch it. She gazed at each of the gargoyles in line. Some of them were old, others were so very young.

The elder continued, "We were honored by the trust the Starwalkers placed in us. You need to understand, when we lose the sky, we..." the elder faltered, fading in the sadness of a memory only she could see.

A hand landed on Betha's shoulder, and she tried to smile up at Sir Samson. "Die. We die within a year. Usually within a few weeks. Flight is a core of who we are, and without it, the will to live simply fades," finished Sir Samson. "I wondered if I was going to find you here." He gave a small nod to Talli. "We never should have blocked the room off. Those who lose the sky should have been given the choice. Our stories say we asked the Starwalkers for help, and they gave us the Sky Stone. It is an honor, and we turned our backs because of the pride of a few, and because so many simply couldn't be bothered to stand up for what was right."

Betha's eyes widened. "So all of these people?"

His hand fell back to his side. "Are dying. Either from

losing the sky or from something else. Infection, internal bleeding, broken wings, anything like that. We don't have healers like the angels."

"Derrik wasn't dying," Betha said. An image of him flying over the fey lands came to mind.

"No, he touched the stone to save his people. He also didn't hear the call, but at that point the only one to have touched and succeeded in a century was Magson. If Derrik had heard the call, he would have been drawn to a single portal. But we didn't have the time to wait. Instead, he went to one that could help his people."

Betha did not watch the next couple of gargoyles touch the stone. Instead, she headed outside, staying away from the line. "They aren't called immediately, then."

"Not usually. This time around, we aren't as certain. In the past, gargoyles were called rarely, just as portals needed them. Now," Sir Samson shrugged, "There must be many portals not guarded since it has been so many years. Many will be called. It is our duty. We will see how quickly it happens."

The line kept moving, and it seemed to pick up speed as those farther back caught sight of her. They gave deep nods of respect, along with smiles and waves. The gargoyles were proud to show the Traveler that they would do their duty.

Betha turned to look out over Mountain Hold. It was carved out of the mountain and then covered in a bright, white stone that glowed in the setting sun. Betha stood at the tallest spot in the city. Balconies and ledges appeared like giant steps before her, giving her a view that was to die for. The lowest tier of the city opened to a large training space before the edge dropped off.

"Will you bless the Sky Stone?" asked Sir Samson. He stood beside her, watching gargoyles fly about their business. Some flew in groups chatting, others were flying with groups of little ones, to strengthen their wings.

"I don't know what that means," said Betha as she twisted her fingers. Kyra's warning of her lack of knowledge came back.

"Realistically, we don't either. When a Starwalker visited in the past, they would touch the stone before they left. That is all we know, and even that is really only a legend. Many of the stories were destroyed or only whispered about in secret when the broken leader blocked off the room. He died several years ago, but his changes lingered."

A chant sounded out over the city, and Sir Samson turned in that direction. A group of gargoyles took to the sky, racing quickly in their direction. Betha couldn't make out what they were saying, but they all were saying the same thing.

"To the stone!" came from the group of gargoyles in the sky. The few gargoyles in line moved out of the way, and Betha stepped forward. Sir Samson's hand settled on her shoulder this time, holding her in place. A gargoyle covered in blood held a little one close to her chest. She vanished into the room that held the Sky Stone.

"That's a child," said Betha, turning away from the opening.

"May they taste the sky," whispered Sir Samson. His

hand trembled on her shoulder. Bright light flashed out of the room and a cheer went up. A sigh of relief came from the gargoyle.

"She just sentenced a child to service," whispered Betha.

"They just saved a child from death." Sir Samson's voice was stern. He moved to stare into her eyes. "They will get to fly and grow. Sing happy little songs. Have a partner, maybe even children. When they are older, they might get to protect a portal. Keep the demons at bay. They will get to live." He let his hand fall from her shoulder. "The mother gets to hold her child tonight—don't you take away from that."

"*Are you okay?*" asked Carter. His voice was soothing in her mind. This morning, he had gone to host a training session with a group of gargoyles down in a field below. They all wanted to learn from him. Angie had gone to rest. It was clear she didn't want to head to the highest part of the city that Betha was in right now.

"*It's complicated.*"

"*Remember, each species is different and needs different things to survive.*"

Betha nodded to herself. The sun moved closer to the horizon, and she let it wash over her. She closed her eyes to breathe for a second, centering herself. Talli was nearby, still watching, along with Sir Samson. She knew what they wanted, and part of her wanted to say no. The other wanted to listen to the call coming from that stone. She could hear footsteps on stone and gargoyles taking to the sky.

When she opened her eyes, the line into the circular

room was gone. It was only the three of them on the balcony. The door stood wide open. The remaining sunlight filtered into the room, settling on the stone.

"I'll touch it," Betha said with finality. She moved away from the balcony and entered the room. It seemed so vast from the doorway, carved out of solid stone. Yet, the more she studied the walls, the more she wasn't sure if it was natural stone. The walls didn't look carved, but she wasn't certain how the room would have been formed. It reminded her of clay from her world but this was harder and smoother than cement would be. The closer she got to the white stone in the center, the more she felt the call in her chest. The marks on her wrist glowed brighter.

"*You got this,*" whispered Angie across the bond. Betha had known she was paying close attention to her, and it made her grin.

Betha reached out, and her hand landed on the stone. Bright light washed over her, and the walls lit up. Lines connecting bright spots traced over all of the surfaces. Inside her chest, she could feel the in-between. Betha gaped when she finally saw it—this was a map, or at least part of one, of the in-between. Only a few of the dots were light blue, the rest were white.

So many unprotected portals covered the universe. Or at least the part she could see.

One blue, protected portal flashed—once, twice, then three times. It wasn't a portal she recognized. She hadn't traveled it. Yet, she was pretty sure she knew how to get there somehow. It was at least one world away, maybe two.

Someone entered the room and blocked the light for a moment. Then another hand touched the stone near Betha's.

A gray gargoyle with a slight green tinge to his chest and arms smiled at her. His eyes sparkled. "That is where I need to go."

Betha jerked her hand back, and the connection with the in-between faded. "What?"

"I can hear the call reaching out from where I'm supposed to go," whispered the gargoyle. He wasn't looking at her. Instead, his eyes stared out into space. "He is waiting for me, holding on with all that he has left." He blinked, then realized Betha was staring at him.

"Balin, you will be leaving then?" asked Sir Samson.

Balin smiled brightly at him. "Yes, there is a portal with an old gargoyle who is fading. That is where I need to go."

"You know it is guarded?" asked Betha.

He nodded. "I could hear him. It started on the training field, and I made my way back up here. It took longer than I would like to admit to realize I needed to come back to the stone. I have had very strange dreams of doorways over the last few nights, and of the dragnus."

"We will need to warn everyone what the signs are," added Sir Samson. "This is cause to celebrate, my friend!" The two gargoyles hugged tightly.

Balin turned back to Betha. "He, the Guardian of the portal, spoke to me when I touched the stone. He wants to meet you. He felt you touch the stone. It gave him enough strength to reach out to me."

Betha had no real idea what was going on, but she knew that if a gargoyle had been guarding a portal for hundreds of years, and had given his life in that service, it was the least she could do to try to fulfill his final request. Somehow.

CHAPTER
TWO

The water was hot, and steam floated in the air. The stone dripped with condensation as Angie sunk deeper in the water. She wondered if they had built Mountain Hold here for the hot spring. The pool of water filled most of the cavern. A ledge was carved into the stone, and steps rose out near the door with an area to place any clothing. It was empty in the cave, and she appreciated being away from everyone. Since they had stepped through the portal to the fey wilds, she had been with others. Even when she was healing, someone was nearby. She loved her friends, her chosen family, but sometimes, even she needed some space.

Hot water helped relax her shoulders, and she kept her walls up around her mind. Before they had left camp, the healer had told her to stay relaxed and to not push herself. For once, she was taking all of the advice she could get. Deep inside, she knew something was off. Betha was up at the Sky Stone, and Angie could hear her thoughts if she peeked down the bond. Carter was leading a training session, and she could tell he was connected with Betha.

Both understood that she needed some time alone.

Light filtered down through a hole in the stone ceiling. This city was strange. Whole rooms had been carved or shaped somehow out of the stone mountaintop. From what she had seen, she wasn't sure it had been the gargoyles. To those carved caverns, white stone had been added. She was thankful for the hot mineral spring that she had been offered when she had asked for a place to bathe and think in private.

Her bright eyes slipped shut. That howl echoed in her mind. The one from the shadow plain when she had taken Betha across the battlefield.

Angie jumped, splashing water everywhere. The light streamed down on her as she peered into the shadows. Her apprehension and curiosity toward the darkness were back. The shadows had been her playground since she was a child. Now, somehow, fear had crept in. Angie took a deep breath. She needed to talk to the others about it.

Conflict and fear rippled down the bond. "You got this," whispered Angie. Betha needed reassurance, and so did she. They did have this.

Sweat dripped down her back as she studied the hole in the ceiling. The sun was starting to set—bright yellow with orange streaked across the sky. It was time to head out. And it was time she spoke about the howl, and about how, for the first time since she had manifested, she was scared to shift.

Scared to look into the shadows and see someone peering back.

$\sim$

CARTER HAD RESISTED the urge to follow Betha farther up the mountain. Instead, he had fallen back to his default task of training others. But this training session wasn't about how to fight. Carter moved through the gargoyles, helping those who had been injured figure out how to regain strength. How to feel confident again.

Betha's conversation with Talli and Sir Samson traveled through the back of his mind. Usually, he was more discreet listening in than this. Yet everything had changed when he had kissed her. Fire had burned in his chest, and he'd felt he could do anything. He hadn't wanted it to end. Not kissing her again had been harder than he thought. Carter wanted to wrap her up in his arms and not let go.

His focus came back to the gargoyle in front of him, who was aiming at a target with his bow. The training field was at the lowest point of Mountain Hold. It was dusty since the grass had been worn away by many feet. This area would be a mud pit if it started to rain. The language barrier was hard, but soldiers understood fellow soldiers. He used hand gestures and small words he had picked up, and they each put in the effort to understand and make it work.

The group of five he was working with all had taken injuries to their arms or shoulders. Nothing that wouldn't heal, but before this, they had used spears.

Carter was trying to get them to learn to use the bow. It would keep them distracted, and they would have more than one shot. And even injured, they could practice with light bows until their strength returned. Feeling useful was important for true recovery, which was all in the mind and spirit. The training field was smaller than he would have liked, but they weren't used to setting up an archery field.

The gargoyles weren't a warrior people. They hunted in groups, usually with spears. Some tribes used bows, the ones who lived in the plains far to the south. The mountain gargoyles seemed to favor spears for the bigger animals that roamed the slopes. The fighting against the demons had only happened over the last couple of years, and they had been using their numbers to compensate for their experience. So many gargoyles died as meat shields. He believed the angels could have taught them how to fight better, and he was angry at the leaders of the angelic hosts for not making more of an effort.

Someone tapped his shoulder. Carter turned and found the five gargoyles he'd been working with were grinning at him, pointing to the sky. He peeked back into Betha's conversation. One of them patted him on the back and started talking too fast for him to parse out what he was saying. Some of the words were in English and others were in the gargoyle's tongue. They all laughed, and he was almost positive they were all talking about him and Betha.

Everyone froze as a shout echoed over the air. "To the stone!" All of the gargoyles around him placed their hands over their hearts. As a unit, they turned toward the tallest balcony. A group of gargoyles were frantically flying toward the area that held Betha and the Sky Stone. The hush that had fallen was eerie.

Then everyone was cheering. The men surrounding him went from silent to celebrating in a breath.

"*Are you okay?*" he asked Betha. Up until now, he had tried not to interfere with what she was doing, but he remained connected with her in the back of his mind. Her emotions were all over the place. It was as if her conversation with Talli was happening right next to him.

"*It's complicated,*" whispered through the back of his mind. Her words held so much tension and sadness. Yet, everyone around him was so happy for whatever had transpired up there.

"*Remember, each species is different and needs different things to survive.*"

Samson's nephew Jadon darted through the air, heading toward him. Carter automatically reached out with his arms.

The little gargoyle crashed into his chest, chattering the whole time. "The little bat is healed!" His speech was getting clearer. The young boy had been working on speaking English.

"Little bat?" asked Carter.

Jadon's hands fluttered, and he spoke several words Carter didn't understand. "A small gargoyle," Jadon pointed to himself. "Broken, but now healed."

One of the gargoyles he had been working with replied. "They will fly again."

Carter pieced together what had happened. It made

sense. There had been a child who had been healed with the stone. Betha had a big heart, especially for children. The fact that they would be bound to the stone bothered her.

They would have so much to discuss on the way back to Terra. The elders had been sharing all of the stories of the Starwalkers since they had arrived. Now, tomorrow afternoon, they would be leaving. Carter was thankful. Both he and Angie had hidden their concern about the gargoyles not wanting Betha to leave, but it seemed unfounded.

Hopefully, it stayed that way. They had promised to return to Terra, as James and Kyra had much to explain. But both Carter and Angie wondered how long Betha would be happy on Terra. She could go anywhere, and one world seemed too small to hold the Traveler she was becoming.

CHAPTER
THREE

The smell of roasted meats filled the air along with laughter and good cheer. Betha smiled as she entered. Gargoyles filled the room, sitting on benches surrounding round tables. The dining hall had surprised her with its groupings when she had first seen it; now she loved it. It was so cozy. While family groups had their own spaces in the city, what defined a family varied widely. Groups of gargoyles lived together, and it wasn't always based on parents and children, siblings, or other blood relations. There were groups of young adults who hadn't paired up who all lived in a big building. Others still lived with their parents or in a separate, smaller grouping of young people.

Betha didn't understand the cultural significance of all of it, but she still thought it was beautiful. If she had lived in a city like this when she was younger, there would have been so much help with her mom. During the day, everyone helped everyone. It was such a connected community. The refugees who had come to the city were dispersed within other groups, and everyone helped with the numerous children they had brought with them.

More and more survivors had shown up. Some were looking for help, others looking for family. The reunions were beautiful, though she did catch more and more worried glances at the sky, as though they were wondering if this was all that was left of their people.

"Betha," said Angie. "Come on, we have a table with a few folks." Her friend added silently, *"You can't just stand and stare at people. It's weird."*

Betha's cheeks warmed as she quickly followed Angie to a table. Carter was already there with Jadon. He was such a cute little gargoyle. Jadon poked Carter, who then acted like he was stabbed, which caused a cascade of laughter from the little one. Sir Samson chuckled as the two interact. Carter caught her watching and gave her a warm smile. Food was set out on wooden boards in the center of the table. There was some kind of meat, along with root vegetables and roasted nuts.

Betha learned to just not ask what the food was. It usually tasted good, and she didn't have any problems digesting any of it.

"So, how was everyone's day?" asked Betha. She grabbed a plate and a napkin before adding some of everything. Tension suddenly radiated off of Angie, and Betha turned toward her.

"I'm scared to shift," she whispered to the table.

Betha's stomach rolled, but she quickly put up a wall

so Angie wouldn't feel her anxiety. Angie didn't get scared. Carter's smile faded into a serious look with his eyebrows drawing together, and he gave Jadon a small pat on the head.

"It will be okay, we just won't have me join you in the shadow plane," answered Betha.

Sir Samson nodded at Carter, then whispered something to his nephew. Jadon gave everyone a smile, then darted into the air and headed toward a gaggle of kids. It was a short flight.

"Why are you scared?" asked Carter. He gripped a wooden cup in his hands as he directed all of his attention at the two of them.

Angie shrugged, then her eyes fell. "It hurt when Betha accidentally burned me. I howled in pain..." She glanced up at Betha. "Something answered."

Betha sat back, her mouth opening slightly. That shouldn't be possible. The shadow wolves were all gone. Then again, Kyra had said she was the only Traveler on Terra, which hadn't been the truth since her and her mom had been on Terra. Kyra didn't know everything and maybe there were other Shadow wolves out there like Betha had been.

"Did they sound dangerous, or did they want to help?" Carter asked softly.

It took a moment for Angie to answer. Betha reached out and slid a hand onto her lower back, rubbing it slightly to support her friend.

"It sounded confused, I'm almost certain. Like, it was shocked to hear me. I didn't respond. Just got us out of there and moved as quickly as possible when we headed back into the shadow plane. The second time it had been just like before—no other voices in the shadow plane." Angie took a deep breath. "What if there are others? They just aren't on Terra..." her voice faded.

"Then we will deal with it when it comes up," answered Betha automatically. She hated seeing Angie like this. "If you run across someone else, that's good news, not bad. It means you aren't the only one."

Carter nodded. "For now, just be careful when you go into the shadow plane. Treat it like an occupied zone. Besides, you can shift without going into the shadow plane, right?"

"I'm scared to shift," Angie replied in a small voice. "It's more than being afraid of what I might find in the shadow plane. When I tried to shift at the end of the battle, I couldn't do it. I'm afraid that I can't."

Betha pulled Angie into a hug. She rubbed her best friend's back, trying to take the fear away. "All you can do is try. Shifting is part of you. It can't just vanish."

Angie took a moment before she pulled back. Tear tracks sparkled on her face, then she wiped them away.

"Your value is not defined by your ability to shift," said Carter. "You are so much more than that."

Sir Samson leaned across the table, his elbows supporting his weight as he smiled kindly. "Trust in your clan, this pack you have." He motioned to Betha and Carter. "You are an important member of your family."

Angie nodded in response.

"We got this." Betha didn't have anything else to add. Carter had hit the nail on the head, and Sir Samson had driven it home. "This is so not getting you out of the fact that we have to fly to Rock Camp tomorrow."

Carter, and more importantly Angie, chuckled at her weak joke. Betha was not the funny one of the group. That was usually Joey, but he wasn't here, and she was doing her best to get Angie to smile. Her thoughts rested on Joey for a moment, and part of her wished he was here. He always made Angie smile.

"Ugh, I'm not looking forward to getting a lift to Rock Camp," mumbled Angie after putting her head in her arms.

"At least it's shorter than the flight here was from the plains," Betha said, trying to highlight the bright side.

Angie and Betha had been carried from the fighting camp in the south to Mountain Hold. Carter had flown the whole way by himself. From what they knew from various messengers, demons were fleeing this world through any portal they could reach. The fighting was limited, and most of it was being done by the trolls and angels.

Music started up from one of the corners that Betha couldn't see. Someone lightly tapped a drum, and another began on a string instrument. Voices took up a song and pulled her attention away from the table. Things seemed somber for the first bit, then the beat picked up and some gargoyles took to the floor dancing. The little ones took to the air in what seemed like a dance as well.

"It is time to celebrate!" called out Sir Samson. "Angie, would you dance with me?" He held his hand out to her, and Betha held her breath wondering if Angie was going to dance. Angie was a really good dancer and Betha always enjoyed watching her. Angie laughed and took his hand, heading out into the crowd.

Betha found herself at the table alone with Carter. His eyes caught hers and he motioned to the dance floor. "Would you like to dance?"

His voice sent a shiver down her spine. Betha's mouth felt dry, but she nodded. Carter stood up and walked around the table before holding out his hand. Betha took it and gasped as he pulled her close. The smell of pine needles drifted over her.

"For the record, I have no idea how to dance," he said playfully.

Laughter that spilled out of Betha as she pulled back slightly. "Come on, I can show you how to move to a beat." She pulled him toward where gargoyles danced in a large circle. The dancers broke the chain and quickly pulled them in to join them. On her left was Carter, and on her right, a joyous gargoyle. Happiness washed over her as the music continued and they spun into the night.

THE CELEBRATION HAD GONE into the late hours. Carter pulled Betha away from the crowd, and they wandered through the empty hallways. The music was still going on in the dining hall, but Betha didn't mind leaving. Carter's hand wrapped around hers as they walked toward her room. The warmth from that contact filled her. She knew her cheeks were flushed. They didn't say anything as her door came into sight.

Confusion filled her. Betha didn't know if she wanted to invite him into her room, plus she was sharing it with Angie.

Carter paused at her door. "Betha—"

Betha cut him off and pulled him in. Her lips met his, and everything inside her melted. For a second, she worried as he resisted. Then his control failed. His hand cupped the back of her head, and he kissed her frantically back. He stepped forward, and Betha found herself pressed up against the wall, his hand still protecting her head.

Slowly, they both pulled away. It gave Betha a chance to catch her breath. She stared up at Carter. His bright blue eyes glowed in the light of the hallway.

"That was great." Her breath out in a rushed whisper, "I hope we can do that again."

"Me too," said Carter, blushing. "We should get some sleep." He stepped back from her.

Betha nodded. "Yeah, that might be a good idea. Good night, Carter."

"Good night, Betha. Sleep well." With that, he gave her a nod and unsteadily headed down the hallway in the wrong direction with a giant smile on his face.

Betha chuckled to herself with a giant goofy grin and headed into her room. Somehow, she would figure out how to fall asleep.

BETHA STARED AT THE STARS. She was back in her quiet place that reminded her of the in-between. At least here, she had the ground with grass instead of nothingness. Fireflies drifted about, and her thoughts kept switching between the passionate kiss and the Sky Stone.

The old Guardian wanted to meet with her, and it was important. Tomorrow, they were supposed to head back to Terra, but it seemed they now had a detour. Not to mention another gargoyle going with them. One who wouldn't be coming back to Sky World. He would bond with the portal just like Derrik had. And he seemed joyous about it, like Derrik had.

It was all so strange. The Starwalkers had given the gargoyles a way to heal themselves. Sir Samson had said they didn't have magical healers. Everything was herbs, tinctures, and knowledge passed down through mostly oral tradition. Things like broken wings and shattered bones were set the best they could. If they couldn't fly again, according to Sir Samson, they just died. The Sky Stone let them heal things their medicine couldn't, but there was a price.

Yet, they knew the price beforehand, and seemingly accepted it gladly. And it kept wars from spilling over into other worlds. If the gargoyles had kept their oath and continued to bond to portals, the demons might never have invaded this world. They might even have been kept out of other worlds like Terra.

Betha didn't know what to make of all of it. The only thing for certain was that none of this was easy. Life was full of hard choices, and sometimes there weren't good answers, only the best choice among sacrifices.

What Betha wanted at the moment was to get back to Terra and explore this thing between her and Carter, then figure out what being a Traveler really meant. But both would have to wait. In this starry place, she took a breath and accepted that the fates would guide her. As the serenity of the presence just like the in-between reassured her, she knew she would find a way.

FOUR

"How are you feeling about heading home?" asked Angie.

Betha paused in her packing and turned toward her best friend. "I'm not sure. I'm sick of battle, and that seems to be ending here. Or at least for now. Who knows what the trolls are going to do? Carter certainly lit a fire under them." She sat on the bed and pushed her pack away in the bare stone room. The only pop of color was a woven cloth hanging on one wall in swirls of blues and greens. It reminded her of the ocean the one time she had seen it on Terra. "We did what I said I would do, which was help the gargoyles. But it doesn't feel finished. Not really."

"Because of the demons," added Angie.

"Exactly. They are still causing problems on other worlds. Like the troll world." Betha couldn't remember the name of it—it always seemed to slip away. "Right now, there isn't anything stopping them from taking over other worlds. The first gargoyle is feeling the call, and he is going to be going with us, but there are so many portals."

Angie glanced down at her fingers, which were sitting in her lap. "But is that *your* problem? Like, is this something that you, Betha, need to solve?"

The question hung in the air, and it seemed to press down on Betha.

"Who else is going to solve it?" answered Betha in a small voice. "How am I supposed to turn away?" Panic built in her chest, and her breathing sped up. Angie quickly joined her on the bed and pulled her into a hug.

"I wasn't saying that we shouldn't do it," Angie said, trying to calm Betha.

"I know, I know. It's just hard." Betha took a deep breath. "Like, not only Terra, but all the worlds connected to the nexus depend on me, and I don't know who else will do anything if I don't. Obviously, no one else is doing anything now, or it wouldn't be this bad."

"I'm sure I have it in me to cross a few more more battlefields," Angie said, trying to sound confident, but only partly succeeding. "But I don't know how many."

Betha nodded at Angie's statement. "You and me, both. I don't think...no, I know I don't belong on a battle-field. That's not how I can keep doing this. I think I have to solve this in the in-between."

Angie let her arm fall from Betha's shoulders. "That sounded rather final. Are you not coming back to Terra?"

"I will. We promised Grandpappy we would be back. After that, I don't know how long I will be gone, and I don't think any of you can go with me this time."

"Let's get back to Terra first. That's the first step, right?"

"*It better be,*" echoed across the bond from Carter. "*I think we could all use a new change of clothes.*"

Angie and Betha both laughed. As soon as they had made it to Mountain Hold, they had done laundry, but it wasn't the same as back home. They scrubbed their clothes in big bins of water with soap. It hadn't cleaned them the same, and they were all trying to get used to smelling like they lived in medieval times.

"That is for sure. I can't wait to take a hot shower and wash my hair," added Angie. "The mineral baths are nice, but it isn't the same. And how about real coffee? Like a latte or even a hot chocolate?"

Betha grinned. "You know I can't wait for some good coffee. Or pizza with garlic knots."

"*You guys are getting me hungry over here. I'm done packing—need some help?*" asked Carter.

Betha glanced around the room. "I think we are almost done."

"*Good. Sir Samson is waiting on us in the hallway.*"

Betha and Angie quickly finished packing and grabbed their bags. Not that they would be carrying them in the air. Betha was doing her best not to think about the flying, for Angie's sake.

"*Warning, I think there are a few additional gargoyles who heard the call.*"

A sigh escaped Betha before she could stop it.

"Why does the Sky Stone bother you so much? You totally would have had your mom touch it if it could've heal her, wouldn't you?" asked Angie.

27

Betha swung her pack onto her shoulders. It was true. She would have done almost anything to heal her mom. "Why doesn't everyone get healed? Why do they then have to serve? If the Starwalkers could create a stone that heals, why is there a cost?"

"Maybe there has to be. You say some vanish—maybe that's part of the balance. When they vanish, what if that's the energy that is used to heal people? Like the healers back home get really weak after large healings, and they need to recover. Plus, they can't heal everything. The stone could be the same," Angie replied.

"But what about the call?"

Angie shrugged. "It could go back to the balance. This is the first stone you have heard of like this. What if it's the only one? Just like your knife was from a Traveler's bones, what if the Sky Stone is the same? Maybe it's a safety measure, like if a demon used the stone and healed themselves. Well, now they might be called?"

"You have been thinking about this," said Betha.

"Well, you've been fixated on this since we got to the city. You've even been dreaming about it. I would have figured you would be dreaming about Carter. Nope, instead it's a glowing stone."

Betha paused near the door. "You know what I dream about?" She could feel her cheeks heating up.

"Not always," replied Angie, "It's been louder since we got to the city."

"Hopefully, it will go back to how it was before once we leave," said Betha, her cheeks definitely burning now.

"Eh, I don't care. I can usually put up a wall if I can't

sleep. It's a lot like the pack, except I like you more," teased Angie.

"That's 'cause you're stuck with me, sister," said Betha.

"Of course!" Angie replied warmly.

Betha followed Angie out into the hallway, which eventually opened up to a balcony. The whole city was like that, walkways and such opened up so the flying gargoyles could take off. She was glad that the fighting hadn't made it here. While it was protected from any ground attacks, other fliers could land almost anywhere. And it was such a beautiful city, it would have been a shame to see it blackened and broken by war.

"Is everyone ready?" asked Sir Samson. His voice was loud to be heard over the crowd. At least ten gargoyles were in a group on the balcony, plus Carter. There were more gargoyles than she had thought were going.

Balin stood next to Carter. "Starwalker," he bowed his head. "We are all ready to serve."

Panic bubbled up again inside of her. These gargoyles were all going to vanish into the bonds with portals throughout the in-between.

"Deep breaths," whispered Carter, suddenly by her side.

Balin watched her reaction, the eyebrows above his eyes drew together. "We chose this. We want this—do not worry. Do not take this service away from us." Others heard what he was saying, and the chatter quieted. Their eyes rested on her. "All things in all the worlds have a purpose. This is ours. We had forgotten it, to our shame, but to find it again brings meaning to our people."

"For our people!" The various voices of the gargoyles called out, their faces joyous. Betha nodded, doing her best to push the uncertainty away inside her heart.

"To the air," commanded Sir Samson.

Gargoyles jumped upward, and her bag was taken from her hand. Someone scooped Angie up, and Betha watched everyone take to the sky. Carter gave her a big smile, then his wings appeared as he took to the air. Sir Samson moved closer. "Let us join them, Starwalker."

Betha gave him a nod, and then she was in his arms and in the sky.

FIVE

The trolls had beaten them to Rock Camp. Three fires burned brightly in the distance, on the edge of the cliff. Carter dashed ahead with the gargoyles leading the pack. Air moving through his feathers and his hair brought so much joy to him. When his brother had tried to explain what flying had been like, it hadn't made much sense. At one point, Eric had even tried to carry him through the air, but he still hadn't understood.

Now he did.

The time away from Eric and Kellion had been good. Training with Parian gave him a good baseline for what he needed to know without any of the baggage of manifesting so late. He stepped into his own shoes as an angel instead of following in Eric's, or father footsteps. Especially given how notoriously proud his father was. Just like the archangels who he had been trying to not think about for weeks now.

Focusing on the day-to-day helped, but the thought would slip inside his mind unannounced. Why were the archangels watching Betha? There was nothing he could do about it but wait. At some point the archangels would act and things would become clear. Still, it worried him. Keeping that from Betha and Angie had seemed like the right thing to do, but now he knew he should say something soon. Especially since Betha had a feather from one of them.

Smoke rose up, and he swung around in the air to circle down toward the camp. This time, there weren't any tents. Laughter came from Betha, and he wished he could carry her. He wasn't sure his wings could carry her weight yet, though, and he didn't want to try until he knew they could.

"We are almost there, Angie!" called out Betha.

"The ground is getting closer!" Angie's voice was part panic and part relief. If Carter didn't have a bond with her, he couldn't have understood her drastic panic about heights. Heights had never bothered him. And now, he had wings.

Carter waited until the gargoyles carrying Betha and Angie had landed before landing at last. He couldn't imagine giving up the sky. When Sir Samson had mentioned that gargoyles died without the sky, he understood.

Garruk approached with a smile, his horns polished. "Nice of you to join us!" he said as he held out his hand, and Carter quickly shook his forearm. The troll had cleaned up nicely since the battlefield. A small, rough dragnus head had been carved into the leather armor on his chest off to one side.

"Glad to see the travel hasn't been bad," Carter replied.

"Very quiet, but then again, last time so many were in the group. This time we are moving much faster."

Carter then realized that the group was drastically smaller than it had been when he last saw them in battle. The gargoyles outnumbered the trolls, substantially. Only two additional trolls stood nearby, and they looked younger. They were a little smaller than Garruk with heavy wooden clubs on their belts. "Did everyone else stay?"

Garruk bellowed in laughter. "Couldn't get them to move for the world, not with Magnestial so close. They are helping the gargoyles clear out the camp near the portal. The only reason no one has crossed yet is that I made them swear not to cross until we are ready." The troll counted the gargoyles out loud. "This is more than we thought. Why would they be heading to Terra?"

Carter shook his head. "They aren't going to Terra. They are going to bond with portals."

The Troll's eyes flicked to Betha, who was patting Angie on the back near the closest fire.

Garruk leaned closer to Carter and his voice came out gently. "It shook her, that gargoyle vanishing to protect the portal to Magnestial. Will she be okay with this many?"

"I'll be okay," answered Betha, joining the two of them. "Everyone has a purpose, and not all of them are as noble as this." She took a breath. "I don't need to like it, but I get it. Just like eventually the trolls will be going through that portal to reclaim their homeland, and some will die." Carter didn't say anything, but he noticed the catch in her voice. People dying or vanishing bothered her, but she was trying. That was all he could encourage.

"Someday, Traveler, we will, and it will be glorious. If the fates are on our side, hopefully sooner rather than later. We won't rush it. This is a long hunt, one we all want to go successfully the first time," explained Garruk. "What matters is having a good plan."

"That makes sense—you don't want any more bloodshed than needed." Betha shook her head. "Plus, it won't be over once the demons are gone."

Garruk nodded solemnly and turned toward the direction of the portals that led to the troll's homeland. "We know it will be hard. And it might take decades. But we have time, or we will once it is ours again to help restore the forests and plains."

"You will get there," said Carter. He clapped the troll on the shoulder, even though he was shorter than the green giant. "I hope to see it one day." The dry wasteland and dead trees around the portal came to mind and he hoped for the troll's sake someday the world would heal.

"You will, that I know."

"From what I know, we have plenty of time to see it happen," added Betha. "That's one of the positives about being an anchor."

"There are a ton of positives of being anchored." Carter winked at Betha and wanted to give her a little nudge, but he resisted.

Angie joined the group with a smirk. "You mean like traveling through different worlds, getting kidnapped by demons, and having to go to the tops of mountains?"

"Exactly," replied Carter. "You forgot get to fly, meet gargoyles, and help the trolls regain their homeland."

"May the fates agree," added Garruk. Then reverently, as if in prayer, he said again, "May the fates agree."

Carter looked over the group and felt a sense of pride. They had come so far. When they'd started, Betha couldn't hold a sword, Angie had wanted nothing to do with a bigger picture, and he hadn't really have a sense of family. It was very different now. They were a family, and they had each other's backs.

THEY HAD LEFT EARLY.

Betha didn't know what to think. Most of the gargoyles who had been called were gone. Right at dawn, they just went through the portal, or at least that's what Sir Samson had tried to tell her.

"What do you mean?"

He ran a hand over his face. "They needed to go on their way. Balin waited for you because of the old Guardian, but the rest said they had to go and go now."

The group had shrunk to her anchors, Garruk and his two other trolls, Balin, and Sir Samson. Betha's mouth opened, but nothing came out. They were just gone. She shook her head, not knowing what to say.

"Starwalker, it was time for them to go," Balin's voice was soft as he tried to explain.

"But how do you know that?" she asked.

"We can feel it. Here." He held out his hand, and she grabbed it. "Can you feel that?" His eyes looked hopeful.

At contact with his hand, she could feel something. It was like the stone, but not as strong. It was like a tugging in the center of her chest. "Last night, the tugging increased for almost everyone. They assumed it was because of the demons' movements. We fear they are expanding their territory in a different direction."

Betha hadn't even thought about that. Who knew who was on the other side of the portals? Demons could be all over the place.

"Either way, we need to get down below," added Carter. "Angie and the trolls went down on foot. We need to meet them at the portal."

Betha sighed and held up her backpack. Carter took it along with his own. He stared at her for a moment, then jumped into the air. His wings flashed out of nowhere before they took him upward. Those beautiful white feathers glowed in the morning light.

"He is getting good at that," said Betha.

"Much better than the trip here," said Sir Samson. "It's your last trip with me." He scooped her up and darted after Carter, with Balin following after. She hadn't realized Sir Samson wasn't going through the portal with her, but it made sense. His people needed him, and Mountain Hold was still dealing with refugees. Not to mention all of the children they were trying to reunite with their families and clans.

Sir Samson landed too soon in the clearing near the portal. The trolls weren't there yet, but Betha could feel Angie coming down the trail. To her shock, a giant wolf rushed out of the trees and to her feet.

"You shifted!" Betha exclaimed in joy.

"I did, this morning," answered Angie in her head. *"My paws feel good."*

"That's great news!" Betha glared at Carter as he smiled at them. "Someone could have let me know."

"You mean you couldn't feel her joy in your head at running?" joked Carter.

The truth was that Betha had a little bit of a wall up with the bond, and she had resisted pulling it back. Instead of responding, she just smiled. She hadn't wanted Angie or Carter to know how she was feeling about the gargoyles, or about Carter himself. It was hard enough sneaking glances at him when no one was looking.

"Are we ready then?" asked Garruk, coming out of the trees, the two younger trolls trailing him.

Betha turned toward Sir Samson and wrapped him in a hug. "I will miss you," she said into his broad chest.

"We will miss you too, Starwalker. Thank you for helping my people. You are always welcome in our lands." He took a step back and gave Balin a nod. "Walk with courage and remembrance, my friend."

"I will, sir," answered Balin.

"Let's do this then," added Garruk, walking through the portal with his axe drawn. The two other trolls quickly followed, then Angie darted into the opening. Carter held out his hand as Balin vanished as well. Betha took it, and then stepped through the portal.

"Thank you, Starwalker," whispered Magson in her mind as they appeared in the desert. The sun was setting, and the sudden lack of moisture in the air was stark. Betha hoped her lips wouldn't crack.

And, standing there in the sand, was a demon.

It held up a white cloth. The trolls surrounded it, and Angie paced in circles. Betha quickly dropped Carter's hand as he pulled out his sword. The demon was something like a tropical bird but was dark purple with long talons. And it had a burnt smell to it.

The demon squealed, "Note for the Traveler!" Then it went quiet again.

Garruk turned to look at her. "It was here when we came through. It didn't move. I think that's a truce flag. It repeats the message and doesn't say anything else."

Betha stepped forward. "I'm the Traveler. Where is the note?"

The demon blinked and turned in her direction. It dropped the cloth and a folded paper fell out, hitting the ground. She moved forward, but Carter held up a hand. One of the trolls grabbed it and then backed away, holding it out to Carter.

He took the paper and unfolded it before handing it over. To her shock, she could read it:

Traveler, it seems we might be on the same side after all. Meet me in the Fey Wilds near the river where you were attacked. In turn, I will release three slaves as a gesture of goodwill. All I ask is that you meet and hear me out. I promise I and my companion Typhon will not attack your party. Send a yes or no with the bird. Don't bring more than your anchors.

Betha had to read the note twice. Then repeated it out loud.

"It's a trap," said Garruk. "It has to be."

"They have to keep promises though," responded Betha. "Plus, the slaves are more than likely trolls. She will let them go free." She glanced from the note to Carter, then at Angie.

"Thoughts?" she asked within the bond.

"You can't walk away, so we need to be smart," said Angie. *"But we don't know for certain that they have to keep promises. All we have to go on what the princess said in the dungeon about keeping her word. Keep that in mind."*

Carter nodded.

Betha turned toward the bird. "Tell her yes." The trolls looked at her in shock, while Balin smiled. The demonic bird flew off as the rest of the light faded over the sands.

"It's a trap," repeated Garruk.

"Even if it is, I have to go. You and your companions can head on to Terra. Either way, we need to move. Sir Samson said the sands aren't safe, even at night."

Betha marched forward in what she hoped was the right direction. The last time they had come through the desert, she hadn't noticed much. She'd had a fever and was being carried. Now she could see the shape of tall spiky plants dotting the landscape in the distance near giant rocks. Otherwise, there were sand dunes in every direction.

"You are going the right way," said Angie. The giant wolf marched beside her in the darkness.

"Am I doing the right thing?" Betha asked.

"You had no other choice," said Angie.

"My heart is too big sometimes."

"No, it is the right size for you. That isn't a bad thing."

"Angie is right, this is the right thing for you. You need to be able to sleep at night," added Carter.

The stars overhead sparkled brightly in the darkness. The air cooled down quickly as they walked across the sand. While she could see okay in the dark, it still unsettled her how quiet it was across the desert, like no other living thing existed for miles in any direction.

"The quiet isn't bad. Better than that sandworm," said Angie.

Betha shivered at the thought. She did not want to face a monster in the dark. Yet, it felt like eyes were watching them, despite the quiet. She reached out with her powers to the portal that had to be up ahead. She almost stumbled when she felt it out near the spiky plants. It was guarded, glowing a light blue in her mind. Tears came to the corners of her eyes, and she tried to blink them away. At least one had made it to their calling.

This world didn't have as many tears as Sky World, or even as many as Terra. It also only had a few permanent portals. The two she had already used, plus one other very far away. That one was not guarded.

Betha turned to Balin. "Is this a big world? Does it have a people?" She tried to keep her voice low.

"All we know is that it has the worms. If it has a people, they stay hidden. It is best to travel at night and quickly through the sands, not in the air." That much she remembered from the walk across the sand before—the warning that the air was not safe during the night. Some sort of creature flew in the dark.

"We should move a little faster," said Angie across the bond. The wolf darted forward at a quicker pace. *"I can hear something coming closer, but I don't know what it is."*

Carter whispered something that Betha didn't pick up, and the rest of the group moved faster. The portal to the fey wilds was close, and they slipped through without issue. The sunlight was almost blinding as Betha stumbled forward, trying to reorient herself.

"Where is Tatuk?" asked Garruk.

Betha blinked, looking over the members of the party, but didn't get a word in before Garruk darted back through the portal. Carter took up a position peering down the path, and Angie slipped into the underbrush.

Suddenly, a troll was shoved through the portal, and Garruk followed.

"What were you thinking? You are supposed to be learning how to be a leader!" shouted Garruk. He slammed the younger troll on the back of the head. Tatuk ran his hands over his face sheepishly.

"There was a giant worm thing. I wanted to see it this time. Last time, I didn't," said Tatuk.

"It could have eaten you."

"I was on a boulder."

"This will get back to your mother. She will shame you!"

The troll's face went a lighter green, but he kept his mouth shut.

"Well, we made it here," whispered Betha. "Now we just need to make it out alive."

CHAPTER
SIX

The fey lord tossed in his sleep. Those bright footsteps on his land were back, accompanied by touches of shadows. He had traced their path across his land the first time, and they had stayed on the treaty way to the desert world. Now, they were back, and again were staying on the treaty way. This was confusing—by ancient law, both creatures were free to go wherever was needed, but they stayed on the path. Furthermore, one of the winged Guardians was with them, who also had the freedom to travel anywhere over his land. He fought against the weight of his millennia-long sleep. He moved, twisting within the bark of the tree. Something was happening in his land. He needed to be up.

The lord stretched and twisted. His tree shook, and he felt the birds leave his branches. Their song carried to him even in the tree's depths. A crack appeared, and light filtered into the dark space. His awareness spread across the clearing. Vines raced over the bark growing from the crack in the tree as it grew larger. His hands reached out to either side of the crack, and he shoved. His head and shoulders slipped free as he stumbled to the ground. Silence reigned across the clearing as the bark on the tree healed itself. The lord stood and paused, as still as the surrounding forest giants. Vines peeked out from beneath his dark green hair—the same color as the forest canopy —cascading down his shoulders and across his face. For a moment, his skin felt like bark before turning smooth.

He gazed around the clearing with eyes the same dark brown of the bark he'd just left, then took a step away from his resting place. A multitude of brightly colored flowers turned in his direction and bowed their heads. A soft melody flowed through the air. The vines from his hair spiraled down, and his shape twisted. Dark fur sprouted as he fell onto all fours. Fur the color of the oak's bark solidified with dark green vines growing out of his spine. He sniffed at a smell on the air. Sharp teeth and claws formed as he traced out the scent. He roared as he realized what it was.

The stench of demons was on his land. Something was wrong, and it was his duty to see it made right.

"Carter, we flew this part last time. Do you know how far it is to the river?" Betha was trying to figure out how long it was going to take to get to the princess.

He nodded. "It will take maybe three or four hours of walking. Unless we want to fly again."

Angie shook her great wolf's head no, plus they didn't have enough flyers for that. Walking it was.

"Well, the princess must know how fast we are traveling since she didn't mention a time. I guess we keep going," said Betha.

"We are getting closer to where I need to go," added Balin.

Betha wondered how much farther it was to Balin's portal. She knew it wasn't far off of the fey wilds, since she was pretty sure it was a different one of the hells. The impression she had from Balin was that the elder gargoyle Guardian knew the dragnus, but that was it.

"But it is at least a day's journey, if not longer, before the detour," continued Balin.

Betha didn't know what to say. She needed to talk to the old Guardian, but she also needed to get back to Terra. "Can I?" she asked, pointing to his hand. Balin reached out for her in response.

The route of portals they had to take snapped into place behind her eyelids. The most direct route would involve using a tear here in the fey wilds. After that, Balin's portal was close. Only one or two additional worlds away. Yet, it meant going across what she assumed was a hell world. The tear was much closer to the Terra portal than they currently were. This was different than what had happened last time she had taken his hand—the tugging in her chest was still there, but now they had a map.

"We have some time yet," muttered Betha.

"Wait, are you going off the path?" asked Garruk.

Betha snapped her eyes open to look at Garruk. She let Balin's hand fall.

Carter replied first, "Yes, but not just yet."

"The angels were really clear to not leave the safe zone," said Garruk. "While I don't mind a little challenge, the feathered ones were very clear. And quite adamant."

"Feathered ones," quipped Betha, trying not to giggle. The younger trolls snapped their lips together as well.

"*If it fits,*" said Angie, the laughter clear in her mental voice.

Betha couldn't resist completing the sentence. "*It sits.*" Inside her head, all she could see was an angel trying to sit in a box that was too small. Angie pushed an image her way of a giant cat with tiny little wings, also trying to sit down in a too-small box. But then Betha realized what Garruk had just said. "What's this about a safe zone?"

"I didn't hear anything about a zone. Let's go," said Carter.

The two younger trolls hung back. Garruk nudged them as he passed by. "Tatuk, Maluk, guard the rear and pay attention. The safe zone for traveling the fey wilds." Carter and Garruk pulled ahead talking in a low tone.

Betha stayed in the center with Balin.

"*You going to join us?*" Betha asked Angie.

"*Nope, sticking to the underbrush. I smell demons.*"

The last journey through the fey lands had been relatively demon free. Only once did they have problems. Still, so much had changed since then. Who knew what the demons were up to now? Not to mention, the princess seemed to believe they were on the same side and wanted to trade information. It didn't make sense.

The more she pushed out with her power, the more she could feel tears in the fey wilds. Plus, additional portals. Many more than she had guessed. From her crash course in interworld economics, she had learned most of the goods imported to Terra from various worlds came through here. The fey wilds was a crossroad of sorts, connected to many others and providing a bigger network between worlds. Now she could reach farther and feel the various connections directly, as she learned how to use her powers. Some of which were guarded by gargoyles.

"I forgot to ask their name," muttered Betha, thinking of the gargoyles.

"From the last portal?" asked Balin.

"Yeah, I know Magson, Derrik, and Rasika. But I didn't speak to this one."

He tilted his head. "You can speak to them, even bonded?"

"I can, when I touch them or go in-between."

"That's interesting," Balin replied. "Some of the really old stories say that Travelers can pass messages from portal to portal, but there is so much knowledge we lost by blocking off the Sky Stone. It's hard to tell truth from fantasy."

"That sounds like the story of my life."

"But, you are a Starwalker?" Balin asked in confusion.

"I only found out I was one less than a year ago," Betha replied.

"That sounds like quite a tale. Care to share?"

"Can you talk a little slower?" asked Tatuk. "We are learning the language, but it can be hard to follow sometimes."

Betha snorted and shook her head. They were paying real close attention, just not to the surroundings. "I can try. I don't even know that I'm speaking the gargoyle tongue, though."

"That's a Starwalker ability. They can talk to all. I think the angels can as well," said Balin.

"You mean the feathered ones?" snickered Maluk.

"Hey, don't repeat things like that. Garruk is special, which is why he can get away with it," said Tatuk. He turned to Betha excitedly. "Did you see how big he got at the battle?"

Betha nodded. Garruk had charged at the line of demons, then the dragnus. During his bellowing charge, he had grown much larger than he stood now. His axe had looked tiny in his hands. "How did he do that?" asked Betha.

"Garruk is our most powerful leader. He is a warrior. They are special trolls who protect our people. We want to be like him and are in training to lead someday."

"But not soon!" added Maluk. "He must lead our people to our homeland and for many more years after."

"Is that why you're here?" asked Betha. They seemed a little young to have been chosen to go to the gargoyle world and fight against the demons. But she was basing that on how they had been acting and that they only had clubs. The more she watched them, the more she could tell little differences, like they both had less muscles than Garruk.

They both snapped their lips shut.

"They are here because they snuck into the group of us leaving. They are going back to Terra and staying there. For now, they should be working on paying attention to their surroundings," growled Garruk from the front.

"The smell of demons is getting strong. You might want to move those kids to the middle," said Angie.

Betha paused in her walking at the same time Carter did. He spoke first, "Kids, get in the middle with Balin and Betha. I'll take the back." He gave Garruk a nod as he pulled out his great two-headed axe. "Keep your eyes open."

The dot that was Angie in Betha's mind stayed barely off the trail, and Betha could just make out her shadow in the underbrush. It seemed Angie wasn't ready to try moving through the shadows again yet. The path curved just ahead, creating a blind corner.

The loud squawk of a bird caused her to tense her shoulders up. The demon princess's purple tropical bird from before came into view. Garruk paused, and the whole group stopped. Betha could see the princess up ahead, along with another demon. This was not the river where she had been attacked. They had at least a few hours to go. Why was she early?

The princess walked forward, and Betha took a few steps toward her.

"I'll be in the bushes," whispered Angie.

Carter and Garruk moved slightly in front of Betha.

"I apologize for the change of plans, but the promise still stands." The princess motioned toward the demon, who stayed behind. "Typhon, my lieutenant, will not attack. Nor will I, or the bird. There are three slaves tied in the trees over there." She pointed toward a grouping of trees. "Your wolf should be able to get as close as she wants. I just want to talk to you, Traveler."

Betha moved around Garruk and walked forward. The princess's red hair gleamed in the sunlight. Betha prayed to the fates that this wasn't a mistake.

"*They are slaves all right. I know one of them,*" said Angie.

"What did you want to talk about?" asked Betha. Her voice was solid, which felt good. She felt strangely less anxious than she had worried she would. Having all of her friends here to support her helped, but this was still new to her. Making deals with demons wasn't a skillset she'd wanted to pick up.

The princess studied Betha for a moment and then her speech changed to something else. Betha wasn't sure what, but she could still understand it.

"The king has lost his mind. He has demons running around the Fey Wilds guarding portals. This will cause problems with the fey." She paused and shook her head. "Sustained war is not good for our people. I will provide you with his location, and you need to stop him from leaving the world he's in now. How you do it is unimportant—you can stop the portals from working, kill him, whatever, it doesn't matter. Just stop him from leaving."

Betha couldn't believe that the princess was offering her father up on a platter. "How will that help you? Or me?"

"I will take over the demons and pull back the troops.

That's the deal. You take care of the king, and I pull our people back to our current worlds."

"What about the trolls that are enslaved on their own world?"

Typhon moved behind her into view, but Betha didn't take her eyes off the princess.

The princess rolled her eyes at the question. "The troll world is useless. If you want to try to take it, go for it. I don't personally care. It is not one of mine, nor do I think we belong there. But the king thinks otherwise. Until you take care of him, it would be dangerous to try to reclaim it."

"How will you let us know the info?"

"I will send the bird to you, but you will need to move quickly once you have it. Here." She held out a dark purple feather. "It can always find one of its own feathers."

"So you can track me?" asked Betha, not touching the feather.

"This is what I've got, unless you have a better idea. We don't have much time. Too many demons are roaming these lands to kill you."

"I thought he wanted me alive."

"Not anymore." The princess snorted. "He is blaming you for his string of bad luck. He lost the seventh level of hell, and now portals are turning blue all over, and we can't get through them. If you die, he believes it all goes back to the way it used to be."

THE PRINCESS STUDIED the Traveler in front of her. When the Traveler had been in the dungeon, she had seemed more malleable. Now that she was here holding out the Yullon feather to the Traveler, she seemed less so. But this was one of Akeldama's only shots at fixing the mess the King had created, and she had to hope the Traveler would be amenable.

All loyalty to the king in the hells was just gone. Lieutenants had even talked of an uprising, but it all came back to power. Their very nature made it hard to talk about such things, and almost impossible to carry them out.

The orders had to be followed. Always.

If they had more time, she might be able to wiggle free of his bonds, but this? Demons running around the Fey Wilds? That was going to trigger a war with the fey, or even with the fey lord of this land, and they did not need that. Their numbers were already too low from her brother's folly, and now the additional losses from the king's attempt to invade the gargoyles' world. There were rumors he was sending troops to the angelic portal to try to take that world as well, now that things had gone badly in the sky world. It was sheer folly. She needed to take over, and she needed the Traveler to deal with the king. This was the quickest path to take back to sanity.

"Well?" Akeldama waved the feather in the air. "I don't have time for this."

"We need to move. They are almost here," whispered Typhon.

Betha jerked at that, and Akeldama remembered the girl had understood demonic in the cell.

Akeldama let go of the feather and turned away. Betha moved, but the princess didn't even pause, just kept going toward Typhon. "Good luck, Traveler."

Typhon's arms went around her, and she glanced back for a second. The Traveler was holding on to the feather. All her training helped her resist the urge to smile.

There was still hope. The demons might be saved after all.

Then Typhon moved. The group in front of them vanished as the pathway sped by, almost too fast to see. Typhon's arms tightened around her. "That was risky, even for you," he whispered into her hair.

"We need more time, you know that. Even if all she does is distract him, I need to go take the throne."

"You will, Princess. You will."

Guards were posted at each of the portals, just as the king had ordered. Typhon would drop her off before going to his own post. Since he fast traveled, even though there was no way around the king's orders, Typhon could twist it to suit his needs. Speeding from one's current location to a set of other locations was just too useful for information management.

The crown on her head weighed heavily, but Akeldama was feeling the pull back to hell. The original one. It was a new sensation, and it wasn't just coming from the crown. She didn't know what it meant, but she needed to listen. It had started as soon as she had taken the "troll" slaves. The trolls had thought they were pulling a fast one on her by getting the healer and fey out. Yet, the princess had asked about which slaves to grab instead of just grabbing three random ones. It had given the slaves a chance to make a plan. They had done exactly what she hoped they would.

The healer needed to go or die, just like the fey. The fey, she didn't understand. Only, when he had shown up was when things changed with the king. Her father had started to push farther and farther into new worlds, like the gargoyle world. Somehow, the fey had increased his power, but this rapid expansion and war was insane, stretching even the resources of the hells to their breaking point. With those two slaves gone, the odds she could succeed in wresting control from her father increased.

Finally, Typhon set her down. They were near one of their portals in the fey wilds. It led to the Fifth Circle of hell. The goal was to get the king to it and lock him there. Soon. He was still dealing with the Fourth Circle. The slaves were rebelling, and the demons were having a difficult time holding onto it. More and more demons were getting pulled there. They were going to run out of warm bodies.

"When he falls, I want you by my side," the words slid from her lips, and she watched the impact they had on him. Typhon stood taller, and his eyes gleamed.

"I will be there, my lady." He gave her a bow, and she nodded before stepping into the portal. She had to follow the call to the throne.

CHAPTER
SEVEN

The purple feather fluttered through the air, and Betha couldn't help but catch it. Her fingers tightened over it before she could even think. It felt like any other feather. The words the other demon had spoken came back to her, and she spun toward Garruk.

"Shit, he said other demons were on the way! We need to get the slaves freed."

"All right, on it," said Angie.

Carter and Garruk took the front of the line with their weapons out. "This isn't a good place to make a stand," said Carter.

"We cannot attack first," commanded Garruk. "The travel agreement is clear!"

"Heads up, guys, these aren't all trolls," said Angie, her voice coming from the trees.

Betha turned toward the sound. Angie marched out of the trees, naked. A female troll was helping hold up an elf, along with someone that was clearly green. They were a sight to see. The troll had on threadbare clothing, and one side of her face was scarred. She had green eyes instead of brown, which was strange for her people. The elf looked was barely standing. Her hair was cut in jagged bunches like someone had taken a knife to it. The other green being wasn't something Betha recognized. It had thorns running along its arms, and spikes instead of hair.

"I will leave you both here. Thank you for your help," said the green man in a musical, singsong voice. He then moved into the underbrush. Angie moved to follow, to tell him, whatever he was, to be careful of the demons, but stopped as the strange creature literally vanished.

"Let him go. He got the healer out," said the female troll. "And this is his land. He is safer here than any of us."

"Is his magic why all of you looked like trolls while tied to the trees?" asked Angie.

"Yes, it was the plan to remove the healer."

Angie motioned to the elf. "This is Ayda. She's from Red Kill. She's the healer we told you about from the slave quarters. The one who healed Carter's shoulder."

"We made it?" whispered Ayda. "I can't believe we made it."

Angie nodded and then shifted back into her wolf form.

Ayda wrapped her arms around her stomach, tears in her eyes.

"There isn't time for this," said Garruk. He glanced over at the female troll. "Can you fight?"

"With a club, I'm decent. We trained in secret as much as possible."

"Tatuk, give her your club."

"But, Garruk?" whined Tatuk.

"Now!" Garruk commanded.

Everything was happening so fast that Betha was having a hard time keeping up. Carter stayed focused on the path in front of them. The sound of paws on the ground caused everyone to pause and turn. Around the bend, a hellhound appeared. It looked like a giant black dog with spikes growing out of its spine, glowing red eyes, and teeth that were too big for its mouth. After it, a bunch of short, upright imps darted forward.

Despite the onrushing horde, Carter stood stock-still. "We are traveling down this road per the treaty. We want no trouble," he announced. His voice came out firm, but the group of demons did not slow down. Per Garruk, they had access to these pathways because of the treaty the nexus had with the fey lord who owned these lands. These paths were supposed to be neutral territory.

"We will attack if you do not stop." Again, Cartrer's voice was firm and loud, but not shouting. The wind picked up, and leaves rustled along the path. The hellhound crouched down, preparing to jump. Its spines shook in anticipation. The imps kept flying straight for the group, claws stretched out.

"Last chance. We do not want to fight you."

The dog leaped at him, outpacing the imps, and Carter swung with his sword. It flared white, knocking the dog back as white flames devoured it. The imps screamed and moved even quicker. Betha gulped in air as Garruk darted forward. His bulk blocked most of the view, but whatever happened, Carter, Garruk, and Angie took care of the imps quickly.

Then it was quiet.

Betha hadn't moved—not this time. She glanced back at the two young trolls who were standing guard over the elf behind her. Only one had a club. The other had a small knife in one hand.

"We should probably keep going," muttered Betha.

Carter glanced at the trees with Garruk. "We did not want this to happen, and we did not instigate this." There wasn't a response. He shrugged. "Let's get going. We will still need to camp before we reach the portal. We should be as far from here as we can before we stop, though."

Angie moved closer to Ayda, keeping pace with the elf.

Garruk took the lead. "I know where we can camp safely. There are only a few spots on the route that are guaranteed by trade treaty."

"You know a lot about this place," commented Betha to Garruk.

The troll's brows pulled together. "Studying is required to lead your people. I know the treaties with the fey and the right of way. We had to move through here."

"You are the leader?" asked the female troll. She moved through the group to get closer to Garruk.

He nodded and carefully pulled out several necklaces from under his shirt. He held them up with reverence, giving her a clear view of them. One was the tooth necklace Carter had given him. Another had small wooden beads that were painted blue and green in different sizes.

Once she had gotten her fill, he tucked them back under his shirt.

"You will help save us," said the troll.

"Yes, we go to discuss this with the clans now." Garruk nodded once with a proud smile. "What is your name?" He tilted his head toward her as he asked.

"Leina," she said, tapping her chest lightly. "You?"

"He is Garruk, the Axe that Cleaves in Two!" pipped up one of the young trolls. Betha didn't catch which. Garruk chuckled, then caught sight of Leina's face.

Leina took a step back so she wasn't in line with him anymore as they walked. "You are a warrior." Her eyes were wide, but it wasn't clear if it was from fear or something else.

He held up an empty hand, palm facing her. "Yes, I'm in control. I lead my people and others who have banded with us. Like our cousins, the orcs and goblins."

Betha knew something important was being spoken about, but she didn't understand enough about trolls to get it. She stepped closer to Carter. "Well, this is turning out to be an adventure."

He chuckled. "Yeah, I wish Sir Samson had given us more warning about the path we are on. I didn't think about it on the way here. Garruk told me more about the treaty terms, but I've still barely got the basics. The demons shouldn't be attacking people on the road, I know that much."

"We were attacked last time," Betha reminded him.

"True, and that's a big no-no. The fey lords will need to do something about it. I'm glad I'm not a demon. Even the angels don't mess with the fey lords, from what I've learned."

"Well, you are a feathered one," joked Betha.

He rolled his eyes. "Let's just get to the next safe campsite."

Everyone was on guard as they marched down the trail. Despite the attack, nothing else seemed to be amiss. At one point, they found a pool of blood and a trail leading off the path, but no one seemed inclined to follow it. Everyone gave the puddle a wide berth. The on-edge feeling didn't go away for several miles, but it faded with distance from the ambush.

"*There is something in the woods, but it doesn't smell like a demon,*" said Angie to Carter and Betha.

"*Let's not bother them,*" replied Carter.

Eventually, bird sounds began to resume, and the singing flowers resumed their song. Betha relaxed as the tension faded from the whole group. The flowers were a bright yellow that lined part of the trail.

"Is it safe for a quick break?" asked Carter.

"*Yeah, there is a small creek near the trail just ahead,*" said Angie.

Garruk nodded. "This is a resting spot. You can see the flower." He pointed a finger at a green flower that was in the middle of the tree near the creek. It was small, and if he hadn't pointed it out, Betha wouldn't have noticed it. "We can get water and pause, but it isn't a campsite. There are multiple flowers for a campsite that look a bit like a fire."

Betha plopped down on a rock close to the creek. Her feet didn't hurt, but she had gotten very warm in her armor with the sun overhead. When the noise of the forest had come back, she had put away her sword. Now all she wanted to do was relax. The constant walking was tough, but at least her bag wasn't as heavy as it had been on the trip to Sky World. Or at least, it didn't feel that way. Taking sips of her water helped, and sitting in the shade was even better. Angie wandered out of the underbrush and plopped down next to her, panting.

On the last walk through this area, they hadn't been this informed, but Betha wondered if it was just because they had been on such a time crunch heading to Sky World. Regardless, getting back to Terra was a different story. This time, there were more demons about.

"We will get there," said Betha.

"*Of course we will,*" replied Angie. "*We just can't expect it to remain this easy. That demon princess was spooked. Why did she want to make a deal with us to get rid of the king?*"

"I mean, he seems pretty crazy with all of the wars that they have gotten into." Betha ignored the fact that Angie thought this was easy mode. Then again, the only fight they had gotten into, they had taken care of quickly, and no one had been hurt.

Ayda wandered closer to the two of them. "I still can't believe it worked," she said as she sat down carefully.

"How did you guys escape?" asked Betha.

Ayda pulled her shirt to the side—a healed burn covered a small square of skin. "We heard the princess was trying to find three slaves willing to leave, but they needed to be trolls. The elder trolls decided to get me and the fey out instead. We scorched the brands so they couldn't track us, and the fey made both of us look like trolls."

"You made it out, and that's what matters," said Betha, wincing a bit at the burn mark. It must have hurt, but getting out of slavery to demons would be worth it.

Tears came to Ayda's eyes. "Yes, but the trolls will suffer when it's clear I'm gone. The first time the king calls for me to heal the dragnus or someone important..."

"We made that choice," butted in Leina. The female troll stayed standing but turned to face the little group. The club remained in her hands. "The elders decided. While you could heal our people, you were also healing the enemy. The fey needed to go as well. Whatever the king was doing to him was just wrong."

"Betha, what are they saying?" asked Angie. *"This is all in, I think, troll speak?"*

Betha quickly recapped the conversation for Angie.

"What was happening to the fey?" asked Angie, and Betha relayed her question.

The troll shivered, and Ayda paled. "We don't know. The king had him for a long time. No one could remember a time when he didn't have him."

"I think..." Ayda's voice shook. "I think he was eating pieces of him." Her eyes closed. "I had to heal him again and again. The first time, only small bites of him were missing. Like someone cut slices off of him. After I healed him, bigger bits were missing. He wouldn't talk about it, but it was clearly horrible." Her fingers dug into her arms that she had wrapped around herself.

"Demons eat fey?" Betha asked Angie and Carter.

"Not that I know of, but we really don't know much about

demons besides how they attack. What's normal for them is unknown," answered Carter. Out loud he said, "We should keep moving if we want to get to the campsite before dark."

They all got to their feet and moved on, wary of the next attack.

DEMONS WALKED ACROSS HIS LAND, outside of the treaty ways that were established with their king, and they violated the separate agreement he had with the nexus. Anger rose deep inside the beast as he traveled through the forest.

This was a violation.

His rage broke on the first group he literally ran across. His claws tore into their bodies as his vines held them still, no matter how much they struggled. Rage consumed him as his intelligence was pushed back—the idea of questioning them didn't even come to mind. The fey in the forest fled from the path as he decapitated the ones in armor and shredded the imps into pieces.

Blood soaked into the dirt, and the flowers shivered on the side of the road. Small vines trailed across the dirt, pausing before they touched the bodies. The lord watched them, then nudged the meat forward to reach their tiny tendrils. The green vines pulled the bodies off of the trail with ease, deep into the earth. Singing filled the air as the flowers began to consume the offenders.

At the sound of the song, the rage inside the beast settled. He needed to know what was going on. The footsteps of light and shadow moved closer to his location. Whatever they were, he was not going to ask them. Something was happening down the trail in both directions. One group was taking care of the problem and following the rules. The others, he wasn't sure. His claws dug into the dirt, and he reached out with his senses.

Blood. Blood of the gargoyles. Guardian bodies falling to the ground. The fey lord was moving before he realized it. Ahead, he sent out vines to help the winged ones. The demons were breaking the protections he had promised to the Guardians, and their own treaty with him at the same time. Hopefully, he would get there soon enough to stop this.

CHAPTER
EIGHT

Garruk was trying not to stare at the little Traveler. He didn't understand how such a small person seemed to create these ripples across everything. She had saved Terra, then marched off into the fey wilds with only a few people to try to save the gargoyles. She had the bluster to leave without the crew that had pledged to her. Yes, Kyra had explained that Betha didn't understand the honor the trolls had given her. But still, for a small one to be so brave, and foolish, was confounding to him.

But she'd repaid them by finding Magnestial. Their home world. It was only spoken about in songs around the fire. It hadn't been lost to some great calamity as the songs said; it had been taken by the demons. And their people were enslaved by those bastards. How had he not known? Did they know about Magnestial? How could the elders not say anything when he had pulled together people to help the gargoyles? The gargoyles were spoken about in legend as well. Cousins to them. The ones who could fly. Yet they were real.

Now the traveler was making deals with the Princess of Hell to take out the king. What in the fates was going on? Was her faith in the fates that strong? If she believed this was the right thing, he couldn't argue. Look at what she had accomplished already. His people would sing about her for ages to come. And she had no idea. The stories he would be able to tell.

Then his gaze landed on Leina. The female troll had escaped, having seen battle at some point. The scars across her face told a story. One he wished he could ask about. More importantly, she knew what he was. The others in the group did not know what being a warrior meant. Monster, berserker, kinslayer, beast. All words he had been called in the past when his abilities had erupted. The elders had agreed—well, most had agreed—he could learn control. Not many other had believed he could do it.

Yet he had. It was unbelievable to his people. He had fought for his seat on the council, then realized he'd needed a different strength. He'd needed to learn. So he had pushed to learn and then get his people interested in learning and going to the shifter school. His people had needed to progress, and they had come so far. Now, there were more trolls, who might not understand.

"Leina, our elders will be eager to meet you. I just learned of Magnestial and travel to spread the word to our people on Terra. The hope is that we can take back our home."

"What do the stories say of us?" asked Leina.

Garruk hesitated for a moment.

"I won't judge." Her dark green eyes stared into his.

Garruk's voice came out as a whisper. "The stories are broken. The oldest we have are of our home, and we had to flee a great evil. Only a few groups survived the years of travel. We settled on Terra where we regrouped and prospered. It is said that Magnestial is lost to the ages."

"It worked then." A soft smile came across her face. She seemed younger.

"What?"

"Our stories talk of long battles with the demons, and we were losing. We knew we would be enslaved. The elders decided to sneak some of our people out, with the hopes that they would survive and live free. The fates spoke to the elders before our last battle and gave us hope. They spoke of a Traveler who would help free our people and reunite us at last. I'm in training to be an elder, so I know the old stories."

Garruk's eyes landed back on Betha. Again, the Traveler. The fates had foretold her coming. He worried for her. All knew the fates weren't always kind to those called. And yet he hadn't known about Magnestial and how the fates had preserved his people. He pushed the anger and confusion away. Right now he had to focus on getting everyone safely to Terra.

Ayda gave Leina a nod. "Our stories of leaving the fey wilds are like that. We were created by a fey lord who couldn't have children. His magic made us, but creating us hurt him. The fey lord was dying, and we couldn't move anywhere else here. Each of the lands is controlled by another, and we didn't want to swear to another. A portal to Terra saved us." She paused to take a breath, then continued, "Some still wait, saying our lord will return someday. My parents think it is foolishness. He is dead and the elves should remain on Terra."

The wolf snorted, and Garruk understood why. That portal had led to an area controlled by the shadow wolves. The elves had slaughtered them to take the land. The elves were still paying the price for that to this day, a steep price imposed on them by the Accords. They were required to provide healers to the Draft, many more than any other race. It was the balance, to heal the damage they had done. The fey wilds had rejected the elves without their lord to protect them. Or that was what he had been taught. They were of the fey, but not fey themselves. It made his brain hurt to think about it.

"Both our peoples fled, and it sounds like they survived. That is a good thing," said Leina. She leaned toward Garruk with interest. "You are a warrior, with control?"

He bowed his head. "Yes. It took many years, but I can control my magic."

Leina hesitated, then said, "Any who showed signs among us were killed. We couldn't let the demons take them. Or discover the bloodlines."

"The bloodlines?" asked Garruk, leaning forward with interest.

"Of the warriors. We couldn't risk that the demons would breed with them and add those powers to the demonic lines."

The rage contained at his center flickered. His people

were forced to kill children to hide the secret. "They breed with us?" Outrage filled his voice, and he fought to temper it down.

"They breed with whatever they can to produce different abilities. Before they came to Magnestial, their horns weren't as pronounced. Or that is what the elders say."

"They will pay," Garruk said darkly.

Leina shrugged. "Revenge is worthless. Freedom is everything, and now we have a chance at it." She was watching the Traveler. "It has been foretold."

THE SECOND BREAK WAS OVER, and Betha climbed to her feet. She didn't complain. They had more ground to cover, and she felt that they weren't yet free of danger. The party got moving again, keeping the same formation. Garruk in the front with Leina, then Betha, Balin, and Angie, followed by Tatuk with Maluk and Ayda, then lastly Carter.

The singing flowers lined the pathway, even more so than what Betha remembered. It seemed every few feet there was another different colored flower that was singing very softly. The yellow ones were her favorite. It surprised her the first time one of the flowers turned toward Ayda. Whenever she got close to them, they pointed in her direction. No one else in the party. If the elves were actually from the fey wilds, the flowers' interest in her made sense. Yet, Betha didn't understand why they were elves and not fey.

Other flowers were bright red while still others were deep purple. It was the same purple as the feather tucked into her pocket. Trusting a demon didn't feel like the right thing to do, but she wasn't sure they had a choice. The king was definitely causing a lot of trouble, and while the princess might not end up being any better, at least she was willing to talk.

"*It will all work out,*" stated Angie.

"*Why is she helping us?*" asked Betha.

"*I think we are helping her,*" added Carter. "*To take over as queen, the king needs to be taken care of. It's like she can't do it because she seems to have to obey him, or something like that. If we take care of the king, this all ends.*"

"*But it doesn't. The portals still need to be guarded, then this all ends. Plus, they can't do this again as long as the portals are protected. Getting rid of the king is great, but long term, I think the portals are key. The tears need to be fixed so they can't take over all worlds.*"

"*What's the plan then? Right now, we are heading back to Terra,*" asked Angie.

"*I mean, I think that is still needed. I need to talk to the gargoyle that is still holding on, and we need to help Garruk get these trolls home. But after that...I don't think Terra is where we need to be. Or where I need to be, at least.*"

These thoughts had been going through her head since the portals on Sky World had been guarded. Her time near, and especially communing with, the Sky Stone had added to her sense of fate. She and Angie had spoken about it a little, and Betha's place wasn't on a battlefield. Her trying to take down the demon king in a one-on-one battle was not how this was going to end.

Her place was working with the leylines that connected the worlds and healing the tears. Each time she healed a tear, the leylines strengthened, stabilizing nearby portals and encouraging more tears to heal on their own.

"I don't think anyone is expecting you to face the demon king. I mean, if any of us were going to be in that position, it would be me," said Carter. *"I think you are on the correct path though. If you could travel in the in-between, this would be much quicker."*

Garruk slowed down, drawing Betha's attention. Angie stepped forward and joined the two trolls at the front. Anger flowed down the bond from Angie, along with sadness.

"Betha, you don't want to see this," whispered Angie.

All that caused Betha to do was peek around Garruk. Immediately, she pulled back and tried to forget what she had seen. Balin made a gurgling sound, and her attention went to him. Anyone would be shaken seeing body parts from a few of their friends.

"I'm sorry, Balin," said Betha. She moved next to him, wrapping an arm around him. Her focus was on him instead of her own feelings. The tugging came back as soon as she touched him.

"We knew we wouldn't all make it. Most planned to fly as fast as they could at night in the Fey Wilds to get where they needed to go. Some went to the troll world and tried that way." He took a deep breath. "We need to make it Betha. He needs us to."

Betha knew what he meant. The urgency of the Guardian to speak with her was there every time she touched his hand. "Some have made it." She closed her eyes and reached farther out to various portals on this world. "There are ones that are guarded now that weren't. I can see that." At least half of the portals to the fey wilds now glowed a soft blue. The Terra one was still a bright white.

Ayda spoke up. "This shouldn't have happened. The local fey lord shouldn't have allowed it. All answer to them in their lands." Her voice shook as she continued. "This was senseless."

"I'm sorry, but we must keep moving. Or we risk not making it to the campsite," said Garruk. "We can sing for them tonight at the fire." The troll kept his body in between them and the carnage. "The demons will pay for this. They will pay for all of this."

Betha kept her lips snapped shut. Part of her wasn't sure if the demons could be held responsible for any of this. From what she had seen, the demons had to listen to orders as though compelled to. Even the princess had to listen to orders from the king. They could not disobey. It made all of this just so much harder.

It had to stop. Somehow.

SHAME. He felt shame, for he had failed to uphold the treaty. He had failed to protect the Guardians after he had promised them safety in his lands.

Some had died. Not all, but some. Some were too many. He watched from the trees. The Traveler couldn't bear to look at the gargoyles that had been lost. The demons had already been eaten, and the forest would grow larger in this area for many years to come. He had killed many of the trespassing demons, yet he didn't know what to do about the flyers. Part of him still felt like he was still asleep. Forest beast and lord. The contradictions of the fey lords were vast.

An elf was traveling with them. One of his brother's long-lost children. The fey lord that was no more. Lost to the fates because of a folly. A warning to all that came after him—do not tangle with the fates. Protect your lands, your people, and respect the fates. Now a Traveler and Shadow Fen were in his lands, and demons were attacking.

Shame.

He needed more information. What was happening in the world? What had happened while he had slept?

Vines dug deep into the soil, and he let his questions roll across the dirt that his people walked on or flew over. One answered back immediately. The lord struggled to the surface as the beast paced under the trees. Then one of the roses walked out of the bushes, and the lord started in surprise. Only thorns—no flowers or petals—adorned his child. All from his land were his children, and this one had been hurt.

"My lord," The green man sank to his knees. "You have awakened."

The lord inside the beast rose up. He was needed. "I have, just now. What happened to you, my child?" He moved closer to the rose fey, towering over them. His nose sniffed at the small green fey's neck and face. Demons. Yet, he held off the rage. He needed to listen.

"I was taken, many years ago. By the demon king."

Claws dug into the earth and his vines twisted about in the air. Despite his anger, he didn't interrupt the rose fey.

"He ate my flesh and took bits of my power to touch the lands."

The air went still. Nothing moved. No leaves rustled, no bird chirped, and every flower in the forest went silent.

"The troll and elf freed me. The elf healed my body so I could make it home."

The lord rested his massive head next to the rose fey's, and he nuzzled his child. "You are home. No one will touch you again."

A hand reached up and touched him shaking.

The demon king had broken the treaty.

CHAPTER
NINE

The trip to the campsite took the rest of the afternoon even with everyone hustling. Angie kept darting ahead while doing her best not to travel too far into the underbrush. She knew things were watching them. It was clear they weren't demons, since they didn't smell like sulfur, or ash like the hellhounds. More like decaying leaves and thunderstorms. It kept her on edge, but there wasn't anything she could do about it.

She was almost positive it was fey who were making sure they didn't step out of line. When Garruk had spoken of the rules for using the treaty ways, she had listened. It would have been nice to have been briefed on them before they had left Terra, but at least she knew of them now. The rules were simple: don't cause trouble, no fighting, don't harm the trees or the forest, and only stay in areas that are marked for such. If you left the treaty way, your safety was your own concern.

It all made sense, but it would have been good to know. Then again, last time, there wasn't this tension in the forest. At least the flowers were singing again, and whatever was watching them was a good way off the trail. It didn't feel dangerous, either. The dirt path under her feet and the wind moving through the trees felt refreshing, even if eyes were watching them.

Despite the peace, she knew whatever the demons were up to was not good. So much just didn't make sense, and Angie kept trying to piece it together. They had gotten captured by the princess, but now they were making deals with her. Angie understood Betha's point, she would have listened to her to save three people as well. It wasn't a deal a good person could pass up, and of all the things Betha was, a good person was foremost. They all were, really, she had to admit to herself.

Angie moved more quickly down the trail. The sunlight filtered down from overhead, and it would have been a perfect day for a long run in the forest. Not too hot, not too cold. Just right. Maybe the fey wilds didn't have bad weather. She resisted the urge to shift into the shadows. Twice now she had almost shifted into the shadows to range farther ahead, but at the last minute, she had caught herself. Getting over her fear was freaking important. Traveling through shadows was her biggest advantage, and given how things were going, they would need it. Freaking demon kings. She wasn't paying attention and almost passed the tree with the markings.

After skidding to a halt, Angie took a few deep breaths through her nose, trying to smell anything nearby. She could sense anything. Nothing new, at least.

"The campsite is clear. I don't smell anyone around." The

path off the main treaty way had been clear. Not a soul had passed by. Just like last time. Did no one trade with the gargoyles? Or was this way usually unused?

She shook her head. She needed to concentrate as she trotted down the pathway to the clearing. Nothing—no scents, no trace of anyone. It was strange. Her mouth was dry, so she headed to the trees that were blocking her view of the stream. A drink of cool water would help clear her head. It was as it had been before. Fish swam in the moving water, but this time, they stayed away from her. It made lapping up water easier since she didn't need to worry about getting nibbled. Her stomach growled at the thought of fresh fish, but she didn't dare.

"Good, we are almost there," responded Carter. They had some rations packed, and while it wasn't the same as fresh fish, it would do.

Betha's voice trailed through the bond. *"The elf is a little shaken, and I'm not sure what to do about it."*

Angie paused in her pacing around the clearing. The last time she had seen Ayda was with the trolls when she had been healing slaves. While she had hoped they would be able to help the elf at some point, it seemed surreal that they had already crossed paths with her again. Yet, it was definitely the same elf. Ayda smelled the same, and so did her magic. At least the poor girl was now free, and they were bringing her home. Who knew what she had gone through since they had last seen her?

At least Angie and Carter were familiar faces, not to mention the troll. Though the troll didn't seem to want to leave Garruk's side. *"I can stay close. I look scary, and that might be a good thing. If Joey was here, he would have her calm instantly."* Mentioning Joey had just slipped out, and she felt a tug near her heart. She missed him. Not thinking about him had been key on the way out to the gargoyle world. Now they were headed back, and he was slipping back into her thoughts. Soon she'd get to see his smile again.

"Totally. I swear he should go into therapy. Maybe become the first therapy dog with a degree."

Angie chuckled at Betha's comment. *"He mentioned something about psychology before we left. He was trying to keep his options open, and I can totally picture him doing that. It could work well with kids. They love him."* Joey's dog form was special, and children really did love him. Humans felt compelled to talk to him. Most wolves wouldn't agree—they treated him like he was beneath them. She couldn't stand it.

Angie poked her head out down the treaty way as she felt Betha and Carter get closer. If she could have smiled as a wolf, she would. Her two friends were finally seeing each other, and it brought Angie so much joy. A curve in the path blocked the clearing from view of the main walkway. As they approached, she stepped to the side so that everyone could walk down the narrow path to the clearing. Garruk was leading the group, and they looked like an eclectic band of travelers from a fantasy book.

Garruk moved forward with a nod to her as he passed. His green skin blended in with the color of the trees. The troll was interesting. She wasn't sure what to make of him, but he was great in a fight with his huge axe. During the council meeting, he had seemed like someone who only thought with his muscles. But everything she'd seen of him since then had proven otherwise. She wondered why he hid behind the simple facade during the council meeting.

Leina couldn't seem to move away from him. She was following right behind, though her eyes darted all over the place. It was clear she was used to trouble and wanted to be ready for it. The club she had borrowed from one of the trolls was in one hand and she still hadn't returned it.

Betha had an arm around Ayda's shoulder, and Balin walked Ayda's other side, keeping her in the middle. The elf wasn't as pale as she'd been earlier, which was good. More tired and drained than panicky. The two trolls, Tatuk and Maluk, chatted with Carter. Angie stepped back onto the trail next to Ayda, rubbing her side along the elf's leg. Balin had to step back to let her in, but he made room. The elf's hand landed on her shoulder. Angie stuck next to her as they made their way to the clearing.

"*I got this Betha,*" said Angie. "*Take a breather.*"

Ayda's fingers tightened in her fur as Betha stepped away, but then they relaxed. She could do this. She could be a safe person for Ayda.

BETHA WATCHED as Balin helped start the fire with Garruk. Tatuk and Maluk were goofing off, and she swore they had to be kids even though that didn't quite seem right. Ayda sat next to Angie, petting the big, scary wolf. Not that Betha thought her friend was scary. Those golden eyes were perfect as far as she was concerned. Angie was her sister in all the ways that mattered. And she radiated safety like nothing else.

The sky went from being light to dark too quickly, and Betha suddenly shivered. More wood was tossed on the fire and the flames leaped higher.

"I think we get stew tonight for dinner," said Carter as he sat down next to her. "I gave Garruk a few of the freeze-dried rations I had left."

Betha chuckled. "Were you sick of carrying them?"

"I'm glad we had them, and that they hadn't been abandoned at rock camp. It's been good to have them, since we didn't know what was going to happen. Derrik lugged the stuff we had left behind to the plains when he realized something was wrong. I couldn't trash them, though they are very well traveled rations at this point. It would have been a waste, plus the food is still good. I'm glad Derrik thought of that..." Carter trailed off, possibly thinking of their friend. Derrik had been a great companion, someone Betha couldn't have imagined leaving behind. He had fit in with their group, but he'd been on a mission. And that mission had ended with him guarding a portal in his home world.

"Well, this dinner is to him," Carter finally continued. "Without seeing that bonding firsthand, I wouldn't believe it possible. It changed everything." It seemed to Betha that Carter was already having an easier time talking about him, like it didn't hurt as much. Betha didn't know how Carter had accepted Derrik's loss so quickly. At the same time, seeing Mountain Hold and the stone heal people, along with their joy that they could continue to serve, gave her some peace about all of it.

Carter must have found his own way of reconciling some of his grief.

Betha responded, "He was pretty amazing, and now he gets to protect his people. Plus, eventually, that portal will help the trolls take back their world. His story will live on."

The stars flickered overhead, and Betha leaned back on her hands. This world was unique. Each of them was, and there was so much she didn't know. The more places she visited, the more she wanted to see what else was out there. Her excitement was tempered with hesitancy. Each world meant more time away from home.

"You are looking serious now," whispered Carter. She could feel his eyes burning into the side of her head.

"Just thinking about home and what it will be like when we finally get back."

"I want a shower with liquid shampoo," added Angie.

Betha grinned. "I can't wait for a vanilla latte and a warm chocolate chip cookie, right out of the oven."

"Showering and a change of clothes are first on my list," said Ayda. Her voice floated over the campfire. "Washing my hair will also be nice." She and Angie would get along just fine.

"I miss my family," said Tatuk. "I want to get home so I can go through the ceremony to be an adult."

"You will get there," responded Garruk. "Maluk might have a few more years."

She chuckled at that along with everyone else. Maluk's cheeks darkened in the firelight, but the youngster smiled.

Garruk continued, "I'm looking forward to all of that,

and some roasted lamb, and telling the stories to the clans. We lost trolls during the battle, but they brought honor to the clans."

Carter added, "Hugging Eric, and hearing what trouble he's gotten into without me to keep him out of it."

Leina's voice was rough, and Betha couldn't quite make out what she said. Garruk muttered something to her, and she nodded. His voice rose, "Leina wants to see free trolls living in peace."

Silence reigned after that. Balin smiled, staring into the flames, staying quiet.

Garruk got up and set a pot over the fire. "I used the food Carter gave me. We will have stew tonight! A hearty meal to prepare for tomorrow."

Angie took the late watch to let everyone get some shut-eye. In the darkness, even without touching the shadows, she blended in unseen. It had taken a while for Balin to get to sleep. She wasn't sure if it was a sign of everything Betha had been through, but her friend was out like a light. Angie pulled the wall up between them just a little as soon as blue eyes from Betha's dreams had floated down the bond. As much as she teased Betha about her feelings for Carter, she was happy they were finally becoming a thing. She did not want to see anything from Betha's dream, though. Nope, not when the two of them were like her siblings. Plus, it would be an invasion of Beth'a privacy.

The moonlight glimmered overhead, but it still weirded Angie out. The stars weren't right, the night didn't smell the same, and she swore the trees whispered. The signing flowers had closed up moments before the light transitioned from light to dark, but it still wasn't quiet at all. Sounds of leaves moving and small creatures moving in the forest seemed so loud to her. There was no slow sunrise or sunset here. It happened so quickly, like flipping a switch.

It was wrong. Or at least wrong for her.

Once most of the group was asleep, Ayda sat up and moved toward the edge of the campsite. She stayed within the boundaries created by the trees, but she stared intently out into the darkness. Her voice was soft, but it carried on the wind. "The gargoyles deserve a proper burial. They had safe passage through the air, yet they are dead. Is this what this land is like? Broken promises?"

Nothing came from the trees, and Angie was thankful. The elf stayed there another few breaths, then moved back to the fire. She curled up into a tight ball near Balin. Whatever was in the woods was still watching, but from farther away. That let her focus on the narrow pathway leading into the campsite from the main trading path that they were traveling on during the day. She kept her paws off of the main trail, but a little breeze brought the scents directly to her. That helped a lot.

All at once, a smell like something that had sat out in the sun for too long hit her nose. From a different direction, the smell of a bear drifted through the air. Her ears perked up at footsteps on the path coming from the Terra direction, just barely disturbing the normal sounds of the woods. Tension rose into the air, making Angie want to flee, but she held still.

The trees rustled, and dread moved up from her paws to her stomach. Angie pressed herself into the base of the tree she was near. Staying hidden was key. Everything in her prayed she would remain unseen. The fey watcher moved through the forest and headed straight for the sound coming from the path. Angie still couldn't see anything. The trees were too dense.

Finally, the footsteps paused, and Angie could make out something walking upright. It had large, curved horns that glowed in the light of the moon. It glanced around the trees, sniffing the air. The forest creature was so close. Angie didn't know how the horned thing didn't notice the smell of bear.

Some danger sense must have sprung, though Angie couldn't see what triggered it if the beast hadn't sensed the fey before now. The horned creature darted forward on all fours, heading right toward Angie. All of its claws hit the ground, and it jumped toward the opening marking the head of the path to the campsite. It was midair when tendrils shot out of the trees, flashing almost faster than even Angie could track. They wrapped around the horned beast and yanked. The giant form disappeared mid-leap into the thick trees and disappeared from sight. Angie peered into the woods, trying to get a glimpse, but couldn't see the horned creature at all.

The trees rustled some more, and Angie couldn't hear anything beyond that rustling no matter how much she tried. Whatever the forest creature was, it slowly moved back to its spot behind the camp. The feeling of dread lessened bit by bit.

Finally, the dread was gone, and her body shook. Once her shaking ceased, she moved back toward the campfire, each step careful and quiet. Angie walked around the fire twice before lying down with her back toward it, her nose still pointed toward the path. For once, she wanted the light.

"*Are you okay?*" asked Carter.

"*Stay off the path at night, he said. Fuck right, stay off the path.*" She shook, but didn't get up.

"*What did you see?*"

"*You mean what* didn't *I see? It's out there, pacing us, but we have been following the rules. Others aren't, and they aren't making it.*" Angie tried to hide her anxious fear from the bond but wasn't sure how well she succeeded.

"*I don't think Parian intentionally misled us,*" Carter responded, likely trying to stay reasonable and calm for Angie's sake, "*but it is clear that those were rules we followed on the way here. It would have been good to know, and I'm glad that at least we know now.*"

"*It feels like most angels aren't super helpful besides Parian. He did give you guys new swords,*" added Angie. "*At least most of the angels we met on Sky World were nice.*"

"*Many myths describe angels as being this spiritual race that helps humans, but they aren't,*" said Carter. "*They are just like any other race. They have their own desires and societies.*"

"*Yeah...just like the fey,*" Angie said. Each group of people they had met were different in their own way, including the ones on Terra. Just like Carter had said. The shifters ran and hunted under the full moon. As a pack, they respected those with power and anyone who could help the pack as a whole. The gargoyles had a magic stone they pledged to for healing, and they guarded portals. It was a respected and honored choice to make. Who knew what the fey were like? They had rules of their own and loved to trade. But at one time, they nearly wiped out the elves and forced them to Terra, or so the stories of the Accords said.

"*Do you want me to take over your watch?*" Carter finally asked. "*I'm not sleeping anyway, it seems.*"

"*Not sure I'm going to get any sleep either, so I'll stick with it for now. I'll let you know if anything else comes up,*" Angie said, settling onto her belly but ready to leap up at a moment's notice if needed.

The great wolf stared up at the stars. Her thoughts changed over to her own people. The shadow wolves were their own race, like the angels. More similar to the Pack, maybe, but not exactly like them, either. And everyone had always said she was a miracle, the last of her people. Was it true? Were there others? What had her people been like? What had been their purpose, and did that purpose still exist?

CARTER SHOOK his head as he walked behind the two adolescent trolls, keeping a very close eye on them. The day had dawned with the same light-switch suddenness as night had fallen the day before, and the whole group had risen, packed, eaten a cold breakfast, and headed out.

The rest of the night had gone mostly uneventfully, with one rather glaring exception. Two hours before dawn, the two young trolls had decided to try to "scout" the main road. Fortunately, Angie had still been alert and noticed when the two quietly climbed out of their tent and began to head toward the path. She'd alerted him to the movement, and Carter had gotten up and quickly woken Garruk.

The older troll had moved faster than Carter would have believed possible, grabbing the two youths from behind before they even noticed him. His glaring eyes and scowl were visible even in the faint reflection of the last coals of the fire, and the two had known they were in trouble. He pushed them back into their tent and stood outside it for the rest of the night.

Carter had been surprised the next morning. Clearly, Garruk had not wanted to wake the rest of the party, but when the daylight switched on, he had turned, ducked into the tent, and yelled for several minutes in the growling language of the trolls. Carter knew that the two were physically mature, probably fully adult by the standards of muscle and bone, but the trolls were deeply invested in an ancient culture driven by ceremony. Their psychology was even bound to it, such that they could be physically very old, but if they hadn't been through the proper series of rites, they would still act like children. Such trolls were usually kept in the villages for menial and simple tasks, taken care of by those who had succeeded in the various rights of maturity.

Clearly these two were hoping to gain adulthood and a place of responsibility in their clan. Just as clearly, they were not making the best decisions, but at least this time disaster had been averted. Carter didn't know what Garruk had said, but when the three of them came out of the tent, the younger trolls looked absolutely crestfallen. They quietly and efficiently packed not only their own tent and gear, but most of the rest of the camp while people got ready for the day's march.

And now they were here, and Carter was keeping an eye on the two. He felt for them, and if they could make it through this trial, he was sure he could help them become accomplished soldiers. They just had to survive. Carter looked around, staying alert. He was also serving as the rear guard. While he didn't really worry about being attacked since they were following the rules, they had been jumped by demons while following the rules the day before, so nothing was granted. And he couldn't believe the gargoyles who had died had broken the rules, either.

Ahead of the two sulking troll youths, Betha stuck with Ayda and Balin. Garruk walked ahead of them, with the female troll glued to his side. She seemed to want to know all she could of the clans on Terra, but couldn't speak of her own people, since Garruk was doing all the talking. It was hard to tell for sure what they spoke of, though, since while Carter knew some of the troll tongue, he wasn't an expert. Angie, of course, walked well ahead of the group, scouting as usual.

Carter caught his gaze trailing to the back of Betha more than once. He traced her dangling hair down her back, noticing the tight muscles of her shoulders and back that came from her combat practice. His eyes drifted farther, watching her hips sway as she walked. He reminded himself he should be watching the road, but a few minutes later, his eyes wandered back. Each time he heard her talking to the elf or the gargoyle, he couldn't resist smiling. They were still dancing around a lot of what they were to each other, but he knew that if he could make her life better, he would, in whatever way possible.

"*How are you doing back there?*" asked Betha suddenly.

Carter jerked his eyes up from Betha's fine hips and replied, rather too quickly, "*Fine, just keeping an eye on dumb and dumber.*"

Her pace slowed and she let the two trolls pass her until she could walk beside him. "We are getting closer to Terra."

"Yep, tomorrow we should reach the portal."

"I'm surprised we haven't run into anyone else on the path. Though Angie says something is following us, keeping us safe."

"That is one way to look at it," he replied. "I would say it is making sure we are following the rules. As long as that remains true, I think we will be fine."

Her lips closed, and her eyebrows drew together. Concern radiated from her. "What about when we need to leave the path?" she asked. "Balin and I need to go through one of the tears."

"You said gargoyles had bonded with other portals in this world, and they must have left the path," Carter replied after a brief pause. "I think it's more that if we get into any trouble, it's on us. Garruk isn't going to leave it no matter what. This pathway needs to remain open for his people to travel back to Sky World."

"I mean, that makes sense, I guess," said Betha. "Angie did say the thing was traveling at night, and that's a different rule. Hopefully, you're right."

Something else came down the bond from Betha, but

Carter couldn't make it out. They were very close, but there was also a wall between them that they both kept up because of their growing feelings. It was the right thing to do, but it was also hard. He hoped it would come down, eventually. For both of them.

"Are you okay?" asked Carter, quietly.

"Just anxious," Betha sighed. The image of the purple feather appeared. "I don't know if I should ditch it or not. What do you think?"

"I wouldn't bring it to Terra," he said with certainty.

Betha nodded. Her face was still off, so he reached out and grabbed her hand. Her eyes lit up, and she gave him a big smile. The anxious feeling vanished, and instead, she felt all warm. This was what he wanted her to feel like all the time. He knew that wasn't realistic, but he would help her feel like this whenever he could.

"Is this okay?" he asked softly, a little anxiety of his own leaking into the bond.

"This is great," Betha said, smiling softly, and his anxiety disappeared. A few of the bricks in that wall between them fell away, and it felt good.

This time, he could make out the happiness that was coming from her. He felt his own smile grow bigger. Hopefully, they had all the time in the world.

All the time in all the worlds.

CHAPTER
ELEVEN

Betha wasn't sure what was waiting for them up ahead, but she knew it wasn't good. The singing flowers had stopped their little song about ten minutes ago. Angie had darted ahead to check out what was going on. The last couple of days of walking hadn't been bad. It had been easier than the journey to Sky World. At least this time she wasn't going numb and feeling like she was losing her mind. According to Garruk, they still had an hour or so until they were within the area near the portal. They had paused for a break while Angie had gone to scout ahead to see why the flowers had gone silent. No one wanted to walk into an ambush, and everyone was at least a little on edge.

Betha nudged Ayda. "You okay?" She had filled the elf in on what had happened in Terra before they had left, and how the clean-up work was going. The hope was she wouldn't feel so out of place by the time they arrived back home. She also was going to introduce Ayda to her therapist. Therapy was something that everyone here could certainly use.

"I bet my family is going to whisk me away. I'll be lucky if I'm around anyone but elves ever again." Ayda twisted her hands all about.

It was clear she was loved. Betha couldn't imagine getting yanked away from her friends without a choice. Ayda clearly loved healing people, but it seemed she had a lot of healing she needed to do with herself. "That's up to you. You get to make your own choices."

Ayda shrugged. "It will be what it will be." Her eyes drifted back down the path, then to the sky. "Did you see the dragnus?"

Betha froze. That wasn't something she had expected to think about today. "Yes, I was there when Garruk pushed it back through the portal."

"That was Garruk?" The female troll inched closer to the two of them at his name.

"Yes, Garruk charged at the demons and somehow he grew." Betha held her hand up in the air, motioning the change in height. "Then the dragnus tried to get through the portal. He shoved it back with his axe. Thankfully, he kept pushing it through the portal so I could close it. How do you know about it?"

Ayda suddenly laughed, but it was a cold sound, not one of joy. "I had to heal him. He now has a deep scar on his snout." She shook her head and wrapped her arms around herself. "The king made me heal him—he was almost desperate. It took so much energy that I thought I was going to die. The dragnus was bleeding so much."

"So not dead then," said Liena.

Ayda shook her head and opened her mouth, but then closed it.

"You don't need to censor yourself here," said Betha.

"Well, the dragnus didn't want to be there. When I healed it, I..." She trailed into silence for a moment, then continued. "It was strange. I could talk to him. He wanted me to let him die. I couldn't do that, but he resisted the healing. When he realized the king would just kill me if I failed, he stopped resisting. He kept picturing mountains, clouds, and a volcano. It was his happy place, I think."

Betha didn't know what to say to that. The dragnus had been terrifying, but if it wasn't fighting for the king by choice, then the fact that he had been injured bothered her. The whole situation seemed to be getting more complicated by the minute. Every time she learned something new, it was more apparent that things were not black and white. The king had slaves working for him, and the dragnus might be one of them. The demon princess wanted to get rid of the king to help her people. Or that's what it seemed like to Betha. She didn't know what the king wanted besides to take over new worlds.

"We have a problem," echoed in her head from up ahead.

"What's up, Angie?" asked Carter.

"For starters, a group of demons surround the portal to Terra. We have a mix of them—hellhounds, imps, and what look to be soldiers. It is clear there has been fighting, and they are keeping anyone from getting here from Terra through that portal. They have been here for a while, but I don't see any

bodies of the Guard. A few bodies of demons are stacked up, but that's it."

"Garruk, can demons interfere with the portal to Terra?" asked Betha. "Like, within the terms of the trade treaty?"

Garruk turned toward her from the tree he was using for cover. "The area around the portal is neutral ground, but we are responsible for keeping it open." He ran a giant hand over his face. "I don't know enough to be certain. I was more concerned with traveling through the Fey Wilds. I'm shocked the angels aren't pissed, though."

"Why would they be? They can go directly through their own portal to the gargoyle lands. I think they only came this way 'cause the gargoyles were with them," said Betha. Her thoughts started to race. The truth was she didn't have to get through that portal. However, Garruk and the other trolls, plus Ayda, did. And she wanted to get Angie and Carter home too, if she could.

"That's correct. We are forbidden from traveling through the heavens without direct permission from an archangel," Balin said, inserting himself in the conversation. "The angels don't need to come this way to get to Sky World. They can go through the heavens."

"I bet I can sneak through them to the portal when it is open," said Angie. *"If that would help, of course."*

"That would require you to go in the shadows," Betha said.

"I need to get over it sometime. Plus, we really need to talk with Terra. We need to know what's going on. With Garruk on this side, we might be able to distract the demons and let some of the Guard break through."

"*It's a good idea,*" added Carter. "*She barely needs to peek out to talk to us. We could get this cleared up quickly if there are forces on Terra ready to strike.*"

"*Well, there are several demons at the portal site,*" added Angie. "*I think we are going to need help from Terra. I don't think I can see all of them.*"

"So is that the plan then?" Betha asked aloud.

"*I think it's a good one,*" said Angie.

"What's going on?" asked Garruk.

"Well, there are several demons blocking the Terra portal. Angie is going to go ahead and get through the portal the first chance she has. We will coordinate with her to make sure you guys make it to Terra."

Garruk huffed. "We can clear out the demons."

While she liked his confidence, Betha could feel hesitation from Angie. She only knew what Angie was reporting. They still had some walking to do to get closer. "We can keep going and see for ourselves. Just be careful. If they are trying to prevent us from reaching the portal, they'll be waiting."

This likely wasn't as simple as it seemed. She was beginning to learn that nothing ever was.

ALL ANGIE freaking needed was for the portal to open back up again. It was currently closed, but the trees nearby had the whole area shaded. All she needed to do was stay where she was and wait.

Waiting was so freaking hard.

Kyra must be having fun teasing the demons. The

portal would flicker up, but no one would go through. Then it would shut down. Sometimes it was so quick Angie didn't even have a chance to move. She was closer now, but after watching for the last twenty minutes, it was clear the demons were getting lax, tired of jumping up each time it opened.

The timing needed to be perfect since she needed to become solid to go through the actual portal. Tension increased across her shoulders, and she readied herself. More footsteps and the smell of additional demons crept across her. That wasn't good.

"More demons are showing up. Be careful," whispered Angie. Though she wondered why she was whispering inside her head. It wasn't like the demons could hear her. Betha and Carter could hear her just fine.

The portal flickered open, and Angie went for it. She sunk into the shadows and moved. She appeared next to the portal at the same time that a bunch of bows came through the space. Arrows shot toward the demons, taking them unexpectedly. Staying low to the ground, she rushed forward. Pain rippled across her back as she crossed into Terra.

Shouts and bright lights greeted her, but the pain didn't stop. Warmth was leaving her body, and all she could smell was her own blood. Before she could stop herself, she shifted back to her human form.

"Hold!" a voice yelled.

"Angie?" someone asked.

"Angie!" Grandpappy's voice was a relief, but she was so very tired. Everything went suddenly dark.

"You need to wake up, Angie. We need to know what's going on," said a voice.

The voice was familiar, but she didn't want to wake up. The darkness was comfortable, and she felt safe. "Angie! Get up now!"

Grandpappy's voice cut through the comfort of rest, and she snapped awake. He rarely raised his voice at her, so it must be important. Angie blinked at her surroundings. A healer was on one side and Grandpappy was on the other. Somehow, she was wrapped in blankets, though she swore she was in the Nexus.

"What happened?" asked Angie weakly.

"You came through the portal and got hit. What were you thinking?" snapped Grandpappy.

"Shit, how long was I out?"

"Not long. Thankfully, we have some healers here."

"More demons are showing up on the other side," sputtered Angie. Her mind raced through what she had to repeat.

"We figured that one out," said another voice.

"Betha and the others are on the over there. I got through so we could create a plan of attack. The demons aren't really watching the path."

"It could work," whispered someone she couldn't see. "If they can distract the demons enough to get just a few guys through, we could get a foothold."

"How far away are they?" asked Grandpappy.

Angie sat up quickly, and the room spun. She held out a hand, and the healer took it, helping the room slow down and finally become more stable. "They were maybe twenty minutes away when I came through. I just need to peek out to speak to them once we know what to say."

"You need to get dressed," stated Grandpappy.

"She needs to *rest*. Her energy levels are all out of sorts. Not to mention that healing was intense," said the healer. "If she wasn't a shifter, her legs would have permanent damage."

Grandpappy's mouth snapped shut.

"Talking to Betha and Carter isn't hard. I can stay out of the way," Angie said. She set a hand on his arm. She would help her friends. She couldn't leave them stranded.

"But after this, you need to rest," he said.

"How is Betha?" asked a female voice.

Angie turned her head, and she caught a glimpse of Kyra. The Traveler was pale and had dark circles under her eyes. Her hair hung in greasy tendrils around her face. Kyra was usually put together so well. Whatever she was doing was draining her, and she wasn't leaving to rest either.

"When I left her, she was fine."

Kyra nodded. "That's good. I'm glad that they didn't convince her to stay."

"No, though I'm not sure she is coming directly here. There is so much going on. You have no idea. She also met your grandmother, and she said 'Hi.'"

CHAPTER
TWELVE

P ain rippled across Betha's lower back before it was cut off as Angie disappeared through the portal. It had taken several deep breaths before Betha felt solid again. Now all she could do was hope that her best friend was okay.

"She has to be okay," reassured Carter.

"I know. I'd know if she wasn't," replied Betha.

It was clear that there were more demons than anticipated. The reinforcements that Angie mentioned had shown up. Everyone was on guard and keeping to the edges of the path as they traveled. Now, the group was keeping out of sight and waiting for Angie to let them know what was going on. It was clear there had been some fighting. Dead demons were stacked up with arrows sticking out of them. A group of imps accompanying a cluster of hellhounds were near the portal.

In addition, there were several upright demons with horns and armor. They were carrying weapons, and a bigger one was issuing orders. It was clear these were trained soldiers. Betha didn't know what the plan was, or even what they could do against a group this size besides being a distraction when it was time.

"Betha," whispered Balin.

She turned toward the gargoyle with a frown. Balin and the two young trolls, with Ayda guarding them, were supposed to stay farther down the path.

"Yes?"

"We need to go." He grabbed her hand before she could say anything. The Fey Wilds vanished behind the force of the call that washed over her. The path to the nearest tear that connected to the demon world blazed in bright light. The tug in the middle of her chest pulled harder.

"Hurry—I don't have much more time," whispered across her mind from the fading Guardian. Balin dropped her hand, and it took a moment for Betha to recenter herself. To her surprise, Carter was next to her when she opened her eyes.

"What was that?" asked Carter.

Instead of answering his question, Betha replied, "We need to go. We're almost out of time."

"What?" he asked in a harsh whisper.

"The portal that Balin needs to go to. The Guardian is fading. He needs to speak to me, and we don't dare leave it unguarded, or that's what I feel. I don't know if we are going to make it." Her hands shook as she looked over the group. Garruk and Leina were on the lookout, and then there was Carter. Aside from those three, they didn't have much in the way of seasoned warriors.

"You need to stay here," whispered Betha. "Help

them get back to Terra." Her mind was made up. This she needed to do as a Traveler.

Carter's eyes narrowed. "You can't expect me to stay here. You need help getting to that tear and then to the portal." She could feel his frustration.

"I think once I touch the tear, I can get us to that portal. Once we get there, I'm going to close the tear, along with any others within reach. That would strand you."

"Betha—"

"Carter, listen. Those," she pointed to the two young trolls, "are basically two kids just graduating high school. Ayda just survived escaping the demons. They need your help. Garruk is awesome, and we have no idea about Leina, but they clearly need you regardless."

He held a finger to her lips.

"That wasn't what I was going to say." Carter gazed into her eyes and pulled her close for a kiss. Then he backed away, his bright blue eyes shiny. "Stay safe. Be quiet. Make sure you come back to me."

Betha leaned forward and captured his lips again.

"I will, I promise," she said. She smirked, then added, "After all, I'm a badass Starwalker who travels between worlds."

Betha pulled away and gave Balin a nod. "Let's go meet this gargoyle." She couldn't look back at the man she'd come to love, or at the rest of the group, or she wouldn't be able to go. Everything inside her trembled at the thought of leaving the path. And the group. Betha gathered her courage and kept going because she had no other choice.

It didn't help that they had to travel a bit since the tear they were heading toward was probably where the demons were coming from. Balin stayed silent and by her side as they walked through the bushes to the shadows under the tree canopy.

Each step required careful placement as they circled around the Terra portal. The sounds of the forest were loud, and after getting back behind the portal, the singing of flowers started up again. Betha had to take that as a good sign. The map inside her head gave them a point to keep walking toward, but it wasn't like they knew what was in between here and there. The underbrush wasn't very thick, but eventually she noticed a trail that led in that general direction.

Balin paused. "Should we follow it?"

Choices. Time was ticking, and on the trail, they could move much faster. They wouldn't need to watch every single step as much simply avoid tripping. A bird resembling a blue jay hopped down the trail and pecked at a leaf. It looked safe.

"Yeah, we can always detour off of it, but it's going in the correct direction. We just need to be quiet," she whispered.

Within a few minutes on the trail, it was clear they were moving much faster and quieter than they had been earlier. Everything inside her strained to hear if anything was headed in their direction. Suddenly, Balin grabbed her hand, yanking her to a stop.

He pointed in the direction they were headed and shook his head. Betha held her breath and realized she could hear something ahead very faintly. Both of them frantically looked around for a place to hide. A small bounder sat next to one of the trees, and Betha pointed at it. She quickly headed that way, careful not to break any branches. As she walked, branches and vines moved out of each of her footsteps, then back into place behind her. The forest was helping them.

Balin yanked his wings in tight and huddled next to her behind the rock and the tree. The sound slowly grew louder. Betha could feel time ticking by, though they didn't really have a choice but to stay hidden. The flowers' song cut off and then suddenly many footsteps passed by. Betha peeked out and caught a glimpse of more demons marching down the trail.

"Carter, at least five more of those soldiers are on their way, with some imps," she sent.

"Good to know," replied her Anchor.

One lagged behind the others, taking its time moving down the trail. It paused where they had left the trail and glanced around in each direction. Its eyes glowed a deep red as it stepped off the path. One moment, the demon was there, its eyes locked with hers. The next, vines wrapped around its head and yanked it in the opposite direction, pulling it away from them. It happened so quickly and quietly that Betha froze. Nothing came from where the other demons had headed.

The vines had been those that had moved out of her way. One sat right next to her foot. Yet, it had taken the demon. It didn't seem like it would do the same to them, and she let her body relax. Whatever the rules were, the demons were breaking them, and she wasn't. That would have to do.

They waited another couple of minutes and then the flowers started up again. Betha nodded to Balin, and they hit the trail again. This time, Betha started jogging down the dirt trail, and Balin followed.

"How much time do we have?" asked Betha.

"Enough, I hope," replied the gargoyle as he kept pace with her.

They had to keep moving at a jog down the trail, she didn't want them to be too late. It was harder to hear anything ahead, but they took the risk. The vines had taken the demon who had spotted them. Maybe they would help them again. They made great time on the trail, and Betha felt hopeful. The glowing tear in her mind was much closer.

Several minutes later, Balin spoke again, his breathing harder. "I think we can make it."

Betha agreed.

The tear wasn't far away now, and as long as she could reach it, they would be fine. Hopefully. Sunlight washed down on them as the trail widened, and Betha took a deep breath. This was going to happen. It would be fine.

The imps guarding the tear were as surprised as Betha was as she ran into the clearing.

Neither Balin or Betha them had heard the demons moving around, but the imps clearly hadn't heard Betha and Balin coming, either. The gargoyle whimpered in fear and almost froze, but they didn't have time to stop.

Bright vines snaked down from the trees and twisted around the imps. Betha reached for Balin's hand and moved as quickly as she could, yanking him behind her.

They had to keep moving. The vines were helping them get to the tear. Her fingers touched the tear, then they were gone.

∼

Nyducrin watched as the king raged. The scales on his snout itched where it had been healed, but he didn't dare move. Already, the gory remains of three bodies were piled up in the clearing. Pieces of meat strung about the area, and it reeked of blood. The dirt clearing in front of the cave was usually very orderly, but not today. The sun streamed down, making the smell even worse.

"Where is he?" raged the demon king.

Magic glowed along his crown that burned a bright red, but the fey man did not appear. It seemed that he had finally gotten free. It was almost impossible, but hope was a dangerous thing, even to a dragnus. Just because one slave had gotten free didn't mean that he would. The brand on the roof of his mouth had been given to him by the king himself when Nyducrin had not yet been fully grown. It was one of the only places the great dragnus' body could even burn, and somehow the king had known that. And that brand carried magic that bound him directly to the king, no matter how much he hated it.

He had been so young. Unable to fly.

But none of that mattered now. Staying still as a stone was one of the only ways not to be harmed. Light flared around the king again as he called repeatedly to one slave or another. Eventually, the king would grow tired of this. There weren't any more demons to rage at since he had killed the ones with him. Finally, a solitary troll showed up, but that was all.

"Where is he? Where is the fey?" the king shouted.

The troll fell to its knees. "I don't know my king. I swear!"

"What about the healer? She isn't coming when I call!"

This time, the troll bowed its head and didn't answer. Red light glowed again from the king's crown, and an answering pulse came from the troll's shoulder.

The reply was ripped from the troll's throat. "Gone— they are gone and will never come back!"

Time seemed to freeze, and Nyducrin blinked in shock. Not one but two slaves had gotten away, and they weren't just any two slaves—these were slaves the king had specific uses for. This had to be intentional. Someone was going to pay, and the dragnus could only be glad it wasn't going to be him. He hoped.

The king screamed, and Nyducrin flinched. Fire washed through the clearing from the king, engulfing the troll. Screams echoed off the stone of the mountain as the fire slowly consumed the hapless slave. The smell made the dragnus' stomach growl. He liked to roast his meat before he consumed it. Nyducrin hoped the sound wasn't too loud.

The flames slowly went out, and the king struggled to catch his breath. He stumbled back to the cave entrance, which was near the rock on which Nyducrin crouched. The dragnus narrowed his eyes. The demon king trembled as he made his way inside the cave. Boulders lined the edges of the dark hole that led deep underground. Ny couldn't get his head inside because it was so narrow. The king's stumbles drew his attention.

He had been weakened.

Interesting. Someone was working against the king, and they knew to get rid of the fey he had been feeding on. It had taken a few years for Nyducrin to figure out where the extra power the king had been getting had been coming from. Now that extra power was gone. He flexed his wings, and his eyes traveled across the sky. If he hadn't been ordered to guard from this rock, he would be flying in the clouds. Instead, he would plan from this uncomfortable rock.

"Clean that up!" shouted the irate king.

Nyducrin rolled his eyes at the order but climbed down from his rock. The bodies needed to be moved. At least it would remove the rotting smell. Somehow, he would kill the king and find his way home. And that would be something he would take great pleasure in.

CHAPTER
THIRTEEN

"*Can you hear me?*"

Carter smiled at Angie's voice. It was good to hear from her. He had focused on the fact that she was very capable instead of worrying that something bad had happened.

"*Loud and clear,*" he replied.

"*Uh, where is Betha?*"

It was a good question, but he had to trust in her as well. They all had to trust one another, though given that Betha had started without much training, it was hard sometimes. But he wasn't worried. Not yet.

"*Another five soldiers are on their way, along with some imps. She is fine, just with Balin,*" he told Angie.

He was positioned to the left of the portal, with the two kids and Ayda close behind him. Garruk waiting to the right of the portal with Leina. The portal was the tip of a triangle between the two groups.

"*We are ready to attack and distract them,*" said Carter. "*Once I give the signal, you guys better be ready. Garruk is going to clear a path to the portal. You guys need to meet him in the middle. We want to scatter them."*

"I will relay that," she said, then her presence in his mind was gone again.

The minutes ticked by, and Carter wondered what politics she was having to deal with. Not to mention who was in the Nexus ready to go. Or at least, he hoped someone was in the Nexus ready to go. All the signs were there that Guards were ready to retake the area. If that wasn't the case, this was going to get messy fast.

"People here are very ready. Try not to get hit." Angie sounded confident, and that was all he needed to know.

"Here we go! Wait for my command!" he said.

Carter stood up slowly and darted forward. His blade glowed white with angel fire. All of the demons turned to look at him in shock. His wings were out, and he screamed. The first demon didn't even get to react before it fell. That set off the rest of the demons, who screamed back at the angel in their presence.

All of the attention turned to Carter, which was perfect. He smiled even wider as Garruk charged. The giant troll was on a roll and cleared the way to the portal, knocking four demons into trees with his wild swings so hard that they didn't even twitch when they hit the ground.

"Now Angie! Now!" Carter sent.

Carter parried a blow from one of the larger humanoid demons and was thankful to hear arrows flying through the air. They could do this. The sound of a big cat roaring echoed across the clearing, and the frenzy increased. A large shape fought its way closer to him as he focused on defense and angel fire. The dark shape was in the form of a large panther, and he smiled. Two of the armored soldiers headed in his direction as he took down another imp.

"Brutis—decided to have some fun?" called out Carter. He hadn't seen the cat since they had helped close the portals on Terra. Having someone you knew nearby was always good.

The responding growl took more focus off of him. The distractions were working. Between Garruk, him, and the friends coming out of the portal, it was enough to create complete chaos. The large demon shouted something that Carter couldn't understand, and the remaining demons focused on retreating past Carter. The big one must be the one in charge, and he'd just ordered the others to fall back.

More and more allies appeared from the portal until Carter was part of that group. He spotted Garruk shoving the two younger trolls and Ayda through the lines and toward the portal. They would be safe now. That had been the goal. He turned back to the fleeing demons to keep the newly reclaimed portal safe.

GARRUK TOOK a deep breath and stayed steady. Carter would give the signal. Then all that mattered was each step to the portal. The soldiers would need a path out to fight the demons, and the kids with Ayda needed one to safety. Leina would guard the rear. She could hold her own in a fight. Or at least, she would give it everything she had. The demons were going to go down. There wasn't another choice. This was the next step in getting his homeland back.

The flame of anger inside his chest grew. Leina would make it to safety. He would meet her people. She would be free! Magic rippled along his skin, and he could feel his body growing bigger. The axe in his hands felt smaller. Each bone along his spine made a soft popping noise.

Bright white light spilled out from Carter's location, and Garruk charged from the shadows. His axe sliced clean through a demon and its armor. The imps scattered at his approach. His broad swings threw their broken bodies into the trees. Most of the demons had turned toward Carter and started off in his direction. This let him cut into the rear guard and any demon who was too slow.

His eyes stayed on the portal as it flickered. A black shape jumped through the portal and landed in the middle of the demons. Garruk chuckled. The Guards spilled forth, the first hesitating and taking a step back when he noticed Garruk's glare. Recognition rippled through the Guards, however, and he charged to meet him in the middle, clearing a safe path. Each swing of his axe either took out a demon or threw one into the trees.

As soon as they had cleared enough of the demons, he turned his back on the portal. "Leina!" His voice was a growl as the group that had been hidden from where he was charged up from behind the rock. The kids and the elf moved quickly across the ground, and Garruk motioned them on.

Leine hesitated as she approached, her eyes growing wide. Her pace slowed, and some imps noticed. Garruk didn't even think, he just moved, blocking the approach of the tiny demon forms. "Go, Leina! Go!"

The imps swarmed him, dashing about, smaller and quicker than the ones in armor. Other Guards came to his aid, helping to pick off the little bastards. More Guards joined the battle, and eventually the demons retreated. A large figure called out to the demons from the path, and they began to flee.

Anger in his chest encouraged him to chase after this commander, but he froze instead. Chasing the leader could help, but he needed to check on Leina. Garruk turned away, shaking his head. Deep breaths caused pain to roll down his spine and he tightened his grip on his axe to hide his shaking hands. By the time he reached the portal, he was back to his normal height.

Then he stood in the Nexus, his eyes spinning about trying to locate the trolls. "Where is she?"

"Garruk!"

His eyes snapped to Tatuk, that freaking kid. He stood next to Leina.

"Are you okay?" His voice was still gruff as he looked her over, noticing some dirt and blood on her cheek.

"I'm fine," she answered in their language.

"Miss, we need your info since you came through the portal," said an officious voice in the human tongue.

"She is with me." His eyes went to the Guard with the clipboard. His steady gaze did not give even a millimeter.

"Sir, who is she? We have a list of everyone who left, and she's not on it."

"She isn't on the list because she rescued herself from the demons."

A medic looked over the elf, though it seemed she was fine to take care of herself. Then Garruk realized Angie was next to the young elven healer. But he swore she had been fighting the demons. No matter, the quick wolf she was.

"But from where?" asked the annoying Guard.

"Put Sky World for now. I need to speak to the clans. If anyone complains, they can talk to me." The frustration in his voice finally hit home, and the Guard stepped back, muttering something about paperwork and disrespectful trolls. Garruk ignored him.

"Kids, come on. It's time to head to the clan lands," he said.

This chaos would have to wait. He needed to see the kids safely back to their mothers and talk to the elders. The protocol could shove it. Everything had changed for his people, and they needed to know it.

"Sir Garruk, can we get a description of the demon who was in charge of the soldiers outside the portal? We need to make sure we keep that space safe," asked a different Guard, this time with respect.

He rubbed a hand over his face, and realization rolled across him.

This was part of the job that he hated, and as much as he wanted to turn away, he had signed up for this. Not to mention, he had to cause an uproar to even be able to leave Terra, since he sat on the council. Turning away questions from the Guard wouldn't look good. And as much as his people needed to know the truth, they would need the help of the Guard and the other races of Terra to reclaim their birthright. This was part of the price of that help, even if they didn't know it yet.

"You have ten minutes, then I need to speak to my elders. Listen well."

CHAPTER
FOURTEEN

Betha let out a sigh of relief as the in-between flowed around them. The tear was right next to her, glowing a dull red in the darkness. Balin's hand shook in hers, and she turned toward him.

"Are you okay?"

"Starwalker..." His voice was filled with awe, and his eyes were large. His grip on her hand did not let up, and she could feel the call much more easily now. Her focus switched from him to the portal that had been guiding him. It was close.

Betha took two steps, then paused. She glanced at the tear they were leaving behind. With her free hand, she touched the edge of it. A quick pull of her power made it snap shut. The nagging sensation she almost hadn't noticed vanished. More tears were nearby, leading into the Fey Wilds, and the need to heal them was added to her internal to-do list. It wouldn't do to leave all of these open, but she couldn't deal with them now.

"Come on, we need to get moving," said Betha. She led him across the darkness, going directly to the portal that pulsed.

"Where are we?" asked Balin in a voice filled with awe.

"This is the in-between. I wasn't sure if I could bring you here, but given that the route in your head connected to this space, I took a chance." Betha did not let go of his hand and had to keep tugging him forward. "Just walk. Try not to think about it too much."

"Think about what?" he asked.

"The floor," Betha replied, keeping her eyes upward. She did her best to ignore the fact that each time she took a step, a steppingstone appeared.

"What floor? We are flying through darkness, Starwalker," Balin said. The awe was now tinged with confusion.

Betha turned toward Balin. "Wait, what? What are you seeing?"

"Branches of light creating pathways to doors. We are flying through them, not following a path. I don't know how you are flying. Is that part of being a Starwalker? That you can fly in this place?" Balin's voice was filled with wonder. Fireflies darted around her, but he didn't mention them. "Oh, I can see him now. He is close," whispered Balin.

Betha turned back to face the direction they were headed. The portal was a light blue. Each step brought them closer, much faster than that one step should have done. It was strange, but Betha brushed it off. It wasn't the strangest thing in this place, and they didn't have all the time in the world to figure this out.

"Ah, Starwalker, you have come," a voice whispered across the space like a breeze through tree leaves. "And not too late."

"We did our best to make it here as quickly as we could, honored Guardian," she replied, trying to show her respect through the tone of her voice.

"Good. The dragnus will be safe then. My promise is not broken." The old voice sighed, as though a heavy weight had been lifted.

"The dragnus?" asked Betha.

"This portal connects this Circle of hell to the world of the dragnus. I'm all that stands between the rest of the dragnus and their ancient enslavers, the demons. A long time ago, I too had touched the Sky Stone, and it healed my wings. Eventually, I heard the call, but I didn't know what it was. In those days, not many were called, but many were healed. It took me too long to ask about the voice I heard. The Guardian here fell. The demons swarmed their world, killing hatchlings and stopping trade to the Fey Wilds. It was horrible, and all my fault.

"A dragnus caught me trying to travel across their lands to the portal. I explained that I wanted to stop the demons. They made me promise that, if they let me pass through, the invasions would end.

"Now Balin is here to keep that promise strong. Balin, you should go through the portal now and see the world that you will be protecting. I need to speak to the Starwalker." As he finished, the old Guardian caused the portal to surge with light, indicating that Balin was safe to travel through.

Balin tugged forward and almost let go of her hand. Betha grabbed on tight and walked with him up to the portal. "Goodbye, Balin. I haven't known you well, but I'm honored to have known you at all."

"Thank you, Starwalker. May I see you again."

He walked through the portal and, as he touched it, Betha let go of his hand. Then he was gone.

"Starwalker, you need to free the dragnus from the king," said the ancient voice of the dying Guardian.

"The black one?" she asked.

"Nyducrin, the only one. He is a prince, stolen as a hatchling just before I took my place here. He was lost for a time, then found by the king before he was fully grown. He has been a slave ever since. The dragnus still tell stories of their lost prince."

"I can try," Betha replied. This was yet another mission, another dangerous task to undo the evil of this mad demon king. Another obligation, but she couldn't refuse the request of this fading Guardian.

"You will succeed. His people are dying without his magic. Tell him you will help get him to Ythe, the world of floating mountains. He should trust you then."

"I hope so. The last time we met, he tried to kill me. He almost succeeded," Betha replied.

"That was the king's doing. The dragnus used to keep the demons in check before they figured out how to control the great wyrms. You will help. The balance has swung more in line since you have shown up. More

Guardians are bonding with portals. The Tree is more stable than it has been for generations. Tears are starting to heal naturally as the Tree regains its health and vitality."

"The Tree?"

"Yes, the Tree of Life. You call them leylines."

The surface of the portal began to shimmer, and Betha took a step back. The voice went silent and then fireflies swarmed. Next to her, a figure with wings took shape within the fireflies. It was gargoyle-like, but the edges were faded. "Oh, to feel my wings again, one last time."

"Wait, what is happening?" Betha asked.

"I get to go to the heart. Can you hear the birdsong and the breeze?" His voice grew lighter as the fireflies spun in tighter circles. Betha could hear something besides their wings. There was a bird's song, sweet and full of joy, and a voice singing. It was soft, and she couldn't make out the words. Everything in her wanted to listen to the song.

"Goodbye, Starwalker. Thank you for all of what you have done and for what you will do."

The fireflies took off in a steady stream heading away from her, deeper into the darkness. The portal glowed brightly behind her, taking on a blue sheen. Balin had done it. He was now the new Guardian, no longer the brave gargoyle she had known. Maybe it was the older the Guardian, the more they could talk. She didn't know, but she hoped someday she'd be able to speak with Balin again.

The dragnus world, Ythe, was nearby, and their portal was guarded. Their prince was missing, and they were suffering without his magic. Who knew how long he had been enslaved? Yet another world suffering because of the demons spilling over from the hells.

They had to be stopped, and she was going to help. But first, she had to get back to the rest of her group. A few fireflies remained near her.

"Can you help me get back to the portal to Terra?"

The glowing bits of light moved in a complex dance as they headed off in what she hoped was the correct direction. As she walked, Betha noticed tears here and there. At each one, she paused and quickly healed it. She wasn't sure where they led, but she didn't recognize the feeling behind them. Brand new worlds to someday discover. Still, the tears didn't belong, and healing them was the right thing to do. "Might as well get it done since I'm here," she muttered as she walked. A few connected to one or another of the hells. They had the same general feel of sulfur as the other tears to the hells she'd been healing since that day so many months ago. Each time she healed one of those, it felt like a victory. "Can't stop me from doing this. I hope it helps, even if only a little."

As before, the more she used her gift, the more fireflies showed up until it seemed the whole area around her glowed. Eventually, the tears near her took on the familiar forest feel of the Fey Wilds.

Finally, a portal loomed in front of her. A small touch to the edge made her smile. She was back where this journey to Sky World had begun. A peek showed her that the demons were gone, and she recognized the armor the Guards wore. Betha stepped through to the Fey Wilds, ready to see her friends and make sure one angel in particular was unharmed.

FIFTEEN

C arter patrolled the path with a few of the soldiers from Terra when the bond in the back of his mind lit up. The patrol walked slowly and nonaggressively down the path. The rules of engagement were clear— they could not attack first. If demons showed up, they needed to be the ones who swung first.

The group turned back toward the portal at Carter's signal, and Carter took the rear guard.

"*On my way back to you,*" said Carter to Betha.

"*You guys were busy,*" she commented.

"*You were gone for several hours. It all worked out. Garruk, Ayda, and the rest of the trolls are on the other side, along with Angie. She hasn't been back here. I think she got clipped when she darted through the first time.*"

The sun shone, and Carter smiled. They had made a ton of progress, and everything had lined up once they'd gotten the Guard through. The demons had retreated far enough that they couldn't even hear them anymore.

"I know how to fix all of this," Betha said into the silence.

Carter almost stumbled on nothing while walking. The group in front of him kept going as he waved them on.

"Really?" he asked.

The loud squawk of a bird caused him to jerk his eyes up from the ground. The dark purple bird rested in the branches of a nearby tree. *"Betha, the bird is here,"* Carter sent, stopping in his tracks. He could feel her start to move toward him down the path, though it'd take her at least ten minutes to reach him.

"You are with the Traveler," whispered a harsh voice. Carter turned from the bird and saw a dim shape in the shadows just off the path. It was the demon that had been with the princess. His armor was pitch black, and he carried two swords. His eyes glowed red as he glanced about, making sure they were alone.

"I am," Carter responded, resting his hand on the hilt of his sword. He didn't really trust this demon lieutenant.

"Good. The king is on the Fifth Circle. The tears have been closing up. He can be trapped there."

"Fifth Circle?" asked Carter. Getting all of the worlds that the demons had taken over straight was going to take some time.

"It is connected to this one. He is readying to come here," replied the demon.

"To the Fey Wilds? Is he insane?" asked Carter.

The demon nodded. "It would mean war."

The bird squawked again, drawing his attention. "It is time. It is time. End this."

He took a step back from the bird. It was creepy.

Carter returned his attention to the lieutenant, but he was gone. Betha jogged down the path with a large panther beside her. The bird took one look at the panther and took off in the air, flying quickly away.

"What happened?" asked Betha.

Carter did a recap, and Brutis growled next to Betha. His skin shuddered, then he shifted into a rather large naked man. "We can't march soldiers off the path into battle to meet the king's forces," said Brutis. Even the patrols could bring conflict with the fey lords, and we do not want to instigate anything with them."

"We don't need to march soldiers." Carter could feel the wheels turning in her head. "I need to get back to Sky World." She reached into her pocket and brought out the bright purple feather. She let it drift from her fingertips, and it floated to the ground. Betha turned back the way she'd come and broke out in a sprint. Carter's mouth dropped, and Brutis shrugged.

"She has grown," commented the cat.

Carter quickly broke into a run, following after her. He answered over his shoulder, "Yep, it's been a journey." He needed to catch up to her before she vanished again.

"Betha? What are you doing?" called Carter after her. All the training and the time on the trail had done her a lot of good. She wasn't going to outrun him, but she had a head start, and he was having to hustle to try to catch up.

"I don't need to go the long way. I can go a shorter

way, I think," she yelled over her shoulder. What shorter way was she talking about? The trip had taken three days just to the desert. Carter increased his speed, sprinting down the trail after her. It wasn't the first time he was thankful he had manifested as he pushed himself to catch the sprinting Traveler.

"How?" he called as he slowly closed the gap.

"Through the in-between," she said.

Betha was going to leave without him. Again. She had vanished already for several hours. Now she was taking off down the trail without taking a moment to even breathe or rest.

"That still takes time," he said.

"Yeah, but not three days of traveling. Time moves differently there, and I can move quicker if I am not closing tears. Closing tears seems to slow time down somehow. At the very least, I need to try."

"I'm going with you!" he shouted as the portal came into view, Betha nearly disappearing into it already.

"What?" She paused before she touched the portal. Carter closed the last few feet, finally catching up to her. "I don't know if that will work."

"We can at least try, but you need to take a break first. You have been gone most of the day. You need food and something to drink. I have your pack stashed with the rest of my gear," Carter said. The concern in his voice was clear, and he saw that she wavered. He pushed his feelings down the bond to doubly make sure she knew he meant well. People were getting hurt, and he knew she couldn't let that keep happening.

"Just grab some trail rations. I can eat as we walk," she said, relenting a little. Her stomach growled.

"Betha..." He hated how his voice sounded pleading, but he didn't know what else to do. Ever since she had tried to rescue them, he wondered what trouble she was going to get into next. Plus, he did not want her going to Sky World alone. It had seemed like the gargoyles hadn't wanted her to leave, but they didn't ask her to stay. If she was by herself, would they try to convince her to stay?

"No, Carter. We finally have a chance to pin him to one world. We need to take it. No more fighting, no more conflict. Heck, I don't even need to see him face-to-face." Betha's voice was confident and direct.

Carter sighed. It was too good of a chance to pass up. Yet, it all depended on the princess giving them truthful information and Betha being able to get everything lined up with gargoyles willing to guard portals.

"Can you really ask gargoyles to bond early to portals to stop him?" He hadn't wanted to ask the question, but he needed to. This all depended on people bonding with portals, ones that weren't called for. It was just like Derrik and his mom had done. It was a tremendous sacrifice, and he wasn't sure she was prepared to ask that of them.

Betha flinched, closing her eyes. Carter grabbed her hand and squeezed it. It took a moment for her eyes to open. "I have to. This isn't just about the gargoyles. I don't want to, but I will." Her eyes watered, and Carter pulled her into a hug, holding her tight.

"All right, let me grab my bag and then we can go." He slowly let go of her arms. "Don't leave without me."

"I won't," she said.

Carter quickly moved over to the pile of stuff to grab the bag that he had carried through all their travels so far. He swung it on his back. Betha stood next to the portal, out of the way. Her hair was pulled back in a braid, and she looked so thoughtful. Within the bond, he could tell she was thinking about something intense, but he didn't want to violate her trust by prying. When she was ready to talk, he hoped she would talk.

"So, what is going to happen here?" asked Carter.

"I'm hopefully going to bring you with me to the in-between. If that doesn't work, then we end up on Terra. I'm pretty sure I know how to make this work, though" she said, with only the slightest quaver of uncertainty.

"Shouldn't we tell Angie what we are doing?" he asked, joining her.

"Is she still on Terra? I didn't feel her when I showed back up."

Carter shook his head. "She got hit heading for the portal, but she made it through, and we spoke to make a plan to get rid of the demons. That was all, though. I have no idea what's going on there now."

Betha's eyebrows drew together, and she frowned. "We better check on her then. I don't want to go traveling without talking to her. With my luck, she would figure out a way to track us down. Or get lost trying to rescue us."

Carter grabbed her hand before she touched the portal, and the two of them vanished.

~

KYRA COULDN'T PROCESS what Angie had said. Time seemed to stop, and it was all that she could do to remain upright. James had appeared from what seemed like nowhere and kept an arm around her waist. The healers couldn't do anything else for her at this point. She had to rest as much as possible and eat to recover her strength.

"My Grammie...she saw my Grammie," whispered Kyra. James pulled her even closer, and she shook. The nexus was anything but empty, with soldiers going back and forth to the fey wilds. The trolls were heading out, and the elf that came through was getting relocated. Kyra focused on James and buried her face in his shoulder. He knew about her family and understood her shock.

At least she was able to stop flickering the portal. Since both sides were now controlled by Terra's forces, she could relax a little, which was good since her emotions were all over the place.

"Kyra, are you okay?" asked Angie.

She pulled away from James, but he kept his arm around her waist. He wasn't going to let go.

"It has been a long week or so. I wasn't expecting news about my family." Her voice sounded unstable even to herself. "It has been a long time since I have seen any of them, and I was really close to my Grammie. Like you are to James."

Angie's golden eyes stared at her, and Kyra wanted to squirm. They were so familiar. Kyra had no idea how James could look at her and not have history slammed back in his face. Every time Kyra saw Angie, the young woman reminded her more strongly of James' long-dead wife. Evelyn had been an amazing woman, and someone that Kyra had called a close friend.

"I can understand that. Not being able to see Grand-pappy would have sucked," Angie replied.

"How is your back?" asked James as his eyes narrowed on Angie.

Angie shrugged. "I'm okay—no more pain, and everything feels pretty normal. I need to talk to you, though. Something weird happened on Sky World when I was running in the shadows."

James' arm went rock solid across Kyra's back, and she peeked at him out of the corner of her eye. His face had gone cold. That was not good, and this was not good timing.

"Like what?" he asked carefully.

Angie paused, seeming anxious, then finally replied, "I heard a howl."

Kyra leaned on James' shoulder. This wasn't going to go well. She had argued that they needed to tell Angie the truth, but he had resisted. Just like he had argued they needed to talk to Betha, and Kyra had resisted. Now it was all going to come to a head. Angie heard a howl, and Betha had met her grandmother.

The fates were having a field day with the two of them, that was for certain.

Looking from Kyra to Grandpappy, Angie added, "And for some reason, that doesn't seem to be surprising to you."

This was not for Kyra to jump into the middle of, and there was no way she was going to say I told you so to

James. "James, are you okay?" she whispered, even though she knew Angie would be able to hear.

"There are too many listeners here," he replied quietly, and Angie nodded.

"We need to talk about it," answered Angie.

"We will. When is Betha coming back? We have all sorts of things we need to talk about," added James. Looked like Kyra was getting dragged under the bus as well. But it was time to clear the air.

"Let me check. Hopefully she's back from her errand."

They followed Angie over to the portal, which had calmed down a bit.

"Her errand?" asked Kyra.

"Yeah, she had to talk to a Guardian and help a gargoyle replace them," said Angie.

The room spun and James was all that kept her standing. His solid arm around her, keeping her grounded. A Guardian? The Guardians were dead. Myths, legends. Bedtime stories told to young Travelers when the weight of what they had to do felt crushing. It was to give them hope that maybe someday the balance would be restored, and they could go home again.

"Guardians?" asked James. It was impossible.

"Yeah, the gargoyles are bonding with portals and stopping the demons from going through."

Kyra shook her head. Gargoyles were Guardians? That wasn't what she had been taught. Guardians were their own thing, weren't they?

"That's news to me," Kyra said. The portal glittered and glowed. Could gargoyles become Guardians? Maybe she would get to be done with the Nexus after all. This needed to end. No matter how she tied the portals to the stone walls within the nexus, eventually they wanted to move back to their original places.

It was taking more and more energy to move them back each time. Supposedly, Guardians helped the portals grow roots into the leylines with portals. If they were real, this could free her.

"I need to talk to Betha—this could change everything with the Nexus," added Kyra.

Angie shoved her dark hair from her face. "Hold your horses. I'll let her know you need to chat. Hopefully, she's back."

CHAPTER
SIXTEEN

They landed on solid stone.

"Oh, shit," groaned Betha.

"I'd prefer if you kept the swearing to a minimum," said a female voice.

Betha spun, still holding onto Carter's hand. A familiar woman stood near them in the courtyard.

"Genessa? This wasn't where we were going," Betha groaned. This was not in-between, and while she knew she had needed to come back to Genessa's home soon, now was not the time. They had to make it back to Sky World to convince gargoyles to bond with portals.

"*Betha, where are we?*" asked Carter through their bond.

"*Genessa's node. This is where I came before, after the dungeon. She is who I told you about,*" replied Betha.

"I assumed not, but a Traveler's promise cannot be forgotten," said Genessa, responding to Betha's spoken question. "You brought one of your Anchors. That is unexpected, but hopefully useful. The terms of your promise were that your Anchors would be safe. You would return when that happened." The older woman raised an arched eyebrow at Betha.

The fact that Angie and Eric were currently safe was a relief, but now Angie really wouldn't have any way of knowing where they were. Just two seconds later, and she could have let her know.

"I was planning on coming back to learn, but I figured out how to stop the demon king. That seemed a bit more important," replied Betha a little defensively.

Genessa smirked. "You are still very young. There is always another problem in all the worlds to be solved. And I already told you, time can pause here if needed. We are outside the normal flow of the leylines. Come." She turned down a path surrounded by rose bushes. "I have tea set out for us. You're here now, so we might as well get through at least some of the confusion."

Betha turned toward Carter as his hand tightened around hers. She could feel the concern coming off of him. "It is safe here," she told him.

"This is strange," muttered Carter.

"I mean, not as strange as some of the things that have happened in the last couple of months. She was helpful last time, and she promised to teach me."

"It just feels like a fairy tale where the evil witch entraps us," Carter grunted, but got to his feet.

"She is a Traveler. I have seen her mark. Plus, without her, I don't know where I would have ended up when I used the knife."

"And she is going to teach you how to use it?" he asked.

"That's the plan," she said, getting to her feet with his help. "Plus, her tea was pretty good last time."

Carter's hand relaxed around hers, and Betha led the way down the path. The smell of roses in the air was such a comfort. She couldn't help but relax. The sky was a light blue, and it felt like a perfect summer day. The bushes trailed off, and the area opened up to a grassy field with a picnic table near the edge of a small pond. Tall trees lined the area, and Betha noticed the cottage she had been in before off to one side.

Genessa stood next to the picnic table. It had several delicate porcelain cups stacked up, along with a large tea kettle. "So where were you trying to head?"

Betha blushed and took a seat at the table. Carter followed beside her. Once they were seated, Genessa grabbed some cups and started pouring tea.

"I was trying to take Carter to the in-between. My goal was to get to Sky World faster. We know where the king is, and if we can get the portals on that world protected, he would be stuck."

"You know about the stone, then?" asked Genessa.

Betha nodded. "Why does it have such a high price?"

"It goes back to the balance." Genessa took a sip of her hot tea. "The energy needed to heal needs to come from somewhere. The ones that can't be healed give what they are to heal those that can. The transfer of that energy makes it easier for them to bond with portals and guard them."

"Yeah, it can be done without it, but it isn't as easy."

Genessa's eyes bore into her. "You bonded someone?

To a portal?" The stern surprise in her voice was unmistakable.

"Yeah, a gargoyle. I helped her touch the energy, I think. That's the best way I can describe it."

"Gargoyles are easy. The fates made them that way. Anyone else is almost impossible, except for Anchors."

"Anchors can be Guardians?" asked Carter.

"Yes. Originally, that is why we bonded with them. Once they bonded with us, we could move that bond over to a portal." Genessa smiled. "Then we discovered the side effects. Taking an Anchor changed us for the better and brought us closer to those people. It made it harder to then help them bond with portals. We asked the fates for help, and the race of gargoyles was created. Those who guard doorways. With the Sky Stone, they can bond without us."

"You are saying I can move my Anchors' bonds to portals?" asked Betha.

"Yes. It is a good safety measure in case someone actually isn't worthy," Genessa said before she took a sip of tea.

"Wait, what?" asked Betha. "Someone has to be worthy to be able to bond with them as an Anchor. That's what Kyra said. Or else, they die." The words tumbled out of her mouth before she could stop them.

Genessa let out a sigh. "This is why I said you needed to learn. If both people are committed, it can work anyway, as long as no one panics."

"But Kyra—"

"Kyra only knows what she was taught before she left for Terra, and she wasn't the greatest student." Genessa set down her cup. "She leaned heavily on her innate abilities. Children are taught the dangers to stop them from bonding before they are ready. Once someone is an adult and ready to bond, they learn more. Kyra never really had that chance."

"You must mean the uncensored version of her past," Betha responded, frustration creeping into her voice.

"Adult Travelers are taught everything about their abilities when they can handle it. History has taught us to be careful, even with our children. A reckless Traveler is dangerous. One who doesn't care about the balance could—and did—destroy so much."

"This isn't the first time I have heard about the balance. What is it?"

"The balance," said Genessa after a brief pause, "is the balance between life, and not."

"So, life and what? Death?" asked Betha.

"Yes and no. Death is a part of life. Death as you mean it is just a change of energy. Your body decays and feeds other creatures. The balance is really about life and, well, more like the absence of life. Life flows through the leylines. The closer a world is to them, and the more well-connected, the more magic that world has. More magic means things like more manifested, more powerful, and more exotic abilities. When a world breaks from the leylines, then you get a shattering. It is the absence of life and light. Darkness like no other. The balance is between these two. You need worlds of life and magic within spaces of darkness."

Betha leaned back with the cup in her hands. "I

mean, how does one even try to upset the balance? That seems so much bigger than the things we do."

"The demons are upsetting it now," answered Genessa. "They are destroying worlds and the unique life on them. Monoculture isn't an expression of life. They are like a sickness. Some of the worlds are starting to go dark. The demons just use them as pathways. They killed or enslaved the populations and moved them off-world. Without life, connections to the Tree fade and worlds die."

It all came back to the freaking demons. Betha shook her head. "I'm going to help stop the king. We have a plan." She wanted to stand up and leave. They had things that they needed to be doing, not drinking tea and learning about balance.

"Calm down," whispered Carter. "This is also important. Either you trust her and time is different here, or you don't."

"Your Anchor makes a good point. What is your name, young man?" asked Genessa.

"I'm Carter of the angelic line."

"You mean you are an angel. I can feel the angel fire burning inside you. You are a strong one. Now that you are here, you will be able to go directly to Sky World. This is my node, and I can make sure you get there," said the older Traveler.

"What is a node?" asked Carter.

"It is a place connected to the various worlds on a part of the Tree. It is a safe place for Travelers and, in Carter's case, an Anchor. We are like the point where twigs meet on a branch. The worlds connect to each other in various ways that are all in the same area. The node connects to them all, and in turn connects the whole cluster of worlds to the greater Tree of Life. It's so things like the demons can't spread beyond certain branches."

Carter nodded, then asked, "Then it's like the Nexus?"

"No," she shook her head. "The Nexus was created by Kyra by bringing portals on your world to one location. Theoretically, any Traveler strong enough can do so to unbound portals. The node was created by the Tree, just like each of the worlds." Genessa grabbed the kettle and refilled her cup. "But that isn't why you are here, and I can tell you are impatient. That comes with youth, I suppose. The knife."

Betha touched that part of her mind that felt like the knife. Her tattoo glowed and then it appeared in her hand.

"You couldn't do that before when you were here," commented Genessa.

"No, it happened after a dream," replied Betha.

"Hmm...Well, the knife lets you touch the in-between wherever you are. Just like when you touch portals and tears. It pierces the veil between worlds. That's how you got here the first time. You touched the in-between, but you were panicking. Thankfully, I yanked you here. You don't want to get lost."

"How would I get lost in the in-between? I just ask the fireflies to take me somewhere, and they lead me there. How do you get lost?" Betha glanced up from the knife in her hand to Genessa. The fireflies always answered.

"Fireflies?" Genessa shook her head lightly.

"Yeah. When I use my power in the in-between, they show up. They are helpful, and they always come," said Betha. Surely the older Traveler knew about them.

Genessa's mouth opened, then closed. Her fingers tapped on her cup. "Interesting. I haven't heard of that before. Usually, when a traveler goes to the in-between, it is pitch black. You need to stay on a lighted trail between worlds, or you can get lost, stranded to wander in the darkness."

"Balin said it was pitch black and he could see the trails. I can focus on them, so I know they're there, but mostly I walk where I need to go. Otherwise, how do I heal tears?"

"Balin was a gargoyle, correct?" asked Genessa.

"Yes, he replaced the fading Guardian that wanted to talk," said Betha, a hitch of sadness in her voice.

"You can heal tears from the in-between..." Genessa's eyes seemed puzzled as she gazed at Betha. "Your mother had a wild story when she stayed here. Josephine said that our seer told her you needed to be on Terra, and that the in-between was calling. Strange."

"The gargoyles call her a Starwalker," added Carter. "I don't know if that is important. They didn't call Kyra one, but I figured it was because they didn't like her much or something."

Genessa's eyes grew wide. "Josephine succeeded then. The fates..." She shook her head as her voice faded.

"What does it mean?" asked Betha.

"Don't you walk among the stars?" asked Genessa.

"I mean, sure, in the in-between," said Betha.

"It's a title, and we all used to be able to do that, according to legend. Once, we could all walk anywhere we wished in that space that you call the in-between. But I haven't known a Traveler that could do that in many years. The gift was taken away by the leylines themselves. Now they're just stories, and the Travelers that remain are bound to the paths between worlds. It just means that you are connected to the leylines more strongly than most, I guess. For now, though, back to the knife."

Betha's hand tightened around the bone in her hand. "It lets me create tears."

"It does, and you must not use it that way. Portals are created by the leylines themselves. Unless they tell you to, don't. It could upset the balance."

"So what do I use it for?" asked Betha.

"As you did before—you can touch the in-between without a portal. You should be able to move to any portal as long as you focus on where you want to go," said Genessa.

"What about other locations?" Betha focused on the in-between.

"Don't use it here!" exclaimed the older woman. Betha dropped her concentration. "This place is formed from the leylines themselves. You could tear them with that. Only use it on worlds." Genessa took a breath and collected herself. "I don't know if it can do anything else. In your hands, who knows? This has been enough today. You will come back and sit at my table again. You still have much to learn, but I have much to think about. And you are still impatient, and young."

Genessa stood up from the table. "Let's get you back on your way." She headed off down the pathway back to the stone courtyard. Betha and Carter followed.

"Carter, what do you know of the seer?" asked Genessa as they walked.

"You mean Andrea? She sat on the council for a long time. It seemed she was really close to Kyra. She betrayed us all to the demons. The fates will deal with her."

Genessa nodded at his words. Betha wondered why she was asking about Andrea. The woman had vanished, was presumed dead, and couldn't mess with them anymore. The change in topic was strange.

Betha added, "We still need to talk to Kyra and the council about her, actually. That's not as high on my list as fixing the demon problem, though."

"I'll take care of that. I don't want to cause an uproar. I can work through Kellion," answered Carter.

"Wait, you mean Kyra doesn't know about Andrea yet?" asked Genessa as she stopped walking toward the courtyard.

Carter shook his head. "We haven't made it back to Terra yet. Angie did, but I doubt she's had time to debrief them on everything that's happened since we left. It's been several weeks. Not to mention, there was fighting in the Fey Wilds outside the portal to Terra."

Genessa's mouth opened, and then she closed it. "This has to stop. I'm putting an end to this."

Betha glanced at Carter. "What do you mean? The

demons? Yeah, we need to stop it. That's what we're going to do."

"No, child. I mean the uncertainty and people operating without enough information. Andrea caused this situation with Kyra. Not to mention she was involved with the demons. It is time to clear the air."

CHAPTER
SEVENTEEN

More and more of the king's favored demons showed up. All full of themselves and willing to do whatever he asked with glee. No orders were necessary. They were laughing, arguing, and making spectacles of themselves. Nyducrin stayed on his rock. It wasn't the first time he had been commanded to stay. It didn't matter how much his stomach rumbled—the binding meant he couldn't even hunt to feed himself. Thankfully there was a tiny spring he could reach from where he was sitting, so he was at least not thirsty.

One by one, the demons lined up outside of the cave. At least twenty high-powered demons, strong warriors who had distinguished themselves in battle. Some of them reported directly to the king, and others, slightly lower in rank, were hoping to make enough of a name for themselves to rise to that most high honor. All were bloodthirsty, nasty demons who wanted war and more death. Surprisingly, none of the high nobles of hell were here. That meant none of those present commanded armies or families. They were all lone warriors. Each wore dark armor and most carried a sword, although some still used claws or talons as weapons.

News had come from a demon who could fast travel —the king had resisted the urge to kill him in anger, and he had fled after reporting in. Tears from the various hells had closed, and some had grown smaller. This was the best news Nyducrin had heard in a long while. If the cracks between worlds were healing, it meant that his world, Ythe, was safer. His ounce of hope grew. The threat that the king would find his way back to his home was so much reduced, now all the dragnus had to do was find his own way back there.

It gave him much to think about. The image of the skies from his home crossed his mind, along with the volcano he visited on this world. Sometimes he could pretend he was home, when he swam in the lava. Someday, he would kill the king and go home.

The noise increased from the group of demons, and Ny focused back on what was in front of him. Finally, the king showed up. His black armor was shined so that it glowed in the sunlight.

The king strolled out of the cave with a manic grin. "My loyal ones have come!" Magic gathered around his crown, but it didn't pulse like it usually did. A red light flickered between the spikes jutting from his head. "It is time to strike. We will spill forth and hunt!"

The demons stomped their feet and howled.

"The Traveler was spotted in fey lands. It seems when one needs something done, they must do it themselves. You have a target! The first one to bring me her body will be elevated to lord and granted the right to start his own bloodline!"

The screams that echoed out from the demons hurt Ny's ears. The lords and ladies of hell were the ones who headed the noble families, granted the right to breed true warriors and build the hordes of hell. Much like the royal family, who they answered to. They were allowed to breed and select traits they wanted to create within their lines. The power to twist their own bodies to perfection came with creating a family. Whoever caught the Traveler would be able to build their own house. It was a great honor, and a new family had not arisen in many generations.

"Go! The hunt starts now!" cried the king.

All of the demons scattered. Twenty or so took off down the trail. Some moved out of sight while others took to the sky. The king took two steps forward, but once everyone else was gone, he stopped. The grin washed off of his face, and the power above his head flickered, then went out.

A lone figure walked the wrong way down the path. Ny narrowed his eyes and realized it was a slave. One of the trolls, beaten and bloody. They strained against the will of the king, but still they walked forward, step by painful step. It was one of the trolls rumored to have magic—one of the king's special projects. He collected any and all who had magic from the enslaved people. Whether they were trolls, orcs, or something else, if they had magic, they had to be turned over to the king. The demon that found them was given more power. Everyone wanted more power. Power let them command other demons with less power and birth new abilities like fast travel. The amount of power a demon had directly tied to its place in the hierarchy of all the hells.

Finally, the troll could defy no longer, and kneeled. As soon as their knees hit the ground, the king attacked. Blood splattered across the dirt as the king ravaged the helpless slave with his teeth and claws. Ny turned away from the feeding frenzy. It was unsightly. One shouldn't make a mess when they eat. Eventually, the sounds stopped, and he flicked an eye open.

"Dump the body with the others. Eat and prepare for battle." The king glared at him, his red eyes glowing with power. Blood covered his face and claws, but he didn't move to clean it off. Instead, he headed back to the cave. "We leave at dawn."

The order rolled across his mind, and Ny's wings spread as he took to the air. His claws wrapped around what was left of the troll as he gained altitude. The crater he dumped bodies in was nearby, and it was close to an area where he could find something to eat as well. He needed to feed if they would be flying toward the nearest fey portal.

Ny poked at the order in his head and tried to fly toward a different area to dump the body. The familiar stabbing sensation took over his limbs, but it was slower to respond than usual. That was different. The order had been weaker.

This was progress. He could use this. He opened his claws over the crater and didn't stick around to hear the body hit the pile of bones.

Angie bounced from one foot to the other. She reached out to the portal and let her senses push outward. Her head was barely through it to the fey side before she tried again.

"Betha? Carter?"

The link with them was still alive in her mind, but they weren't there. It was very strange, something Angie had never experienced before. Somehow they weren't on the fey wilds or Terra. Where the heck did they go?

Angie pulled back, her thoughts racing. Why did they leave without saying anything? Or had something happened to Betha on her trip to the gargoyle world?

"Is she on her way?" asked Kyra. Her eyes seemed bright for the first time since Angie had returned.

"They are gone," said Angie, confused.

"Gone?" Grandpappy's voice was filled with concern. "They can't be just gone. Betha isn't one to not give you a heads-up."

"Things change, Grandpappy. Betha has learned how to stand on her own two feet. Wait until I tell you about how she tried to rescue us from hell." Grandpappy's eyes widened, and she shook her head. "Though this is a little weird, I will give you that. It's not like they just left—it's like they aren't where I expect them to be."

Grandpappy and Kyra moved closer to the portal and the young Anchor.

"I should check with a few guys on the other side to see what they know," said Angie. "That will at least give me a timeline on what happened."

As Angie turned to duck into the portal again, the color flickered within it. Angie gasped, and all of them turned toward the portal. Angie took a step back since she didn't want to block anyone from coming across.

"I can just ask whoever shows up," she muttered. A hand pushed through and landed on Kyra's shoulder. It registered as weird, but Angie didn't have time to respond.

"Grammie?" asked Kyra. The hand took a firm grip of the Traveler's shirt and yanked. Kyra stumbled through the portal, Grandpappy's arm still around her waist. He tightened his grip and stumbled after Kyra, pulled through to wherever the arm had come from. Angie jumped after them as quickly as she could, not wanting to be stuck by herself. The portal flickered around her, and she landed on the ground. There was a reason people didn't jump through portals—they walked. She felt the pain in her knees and wrists as she caught her weight.

"Are you okay?" asked a Guard.

Angie glanced up from the dirt and realized she was in the Fey Wilds. More to the point, Kyra and Grand-pappy were not.

"Oh, fuck!" said Angie.

Her eyes traveled back to the portal she had just left. A hand reached down to her.

"Hey, miss, you good? Traveling can be a little weird," asked a different soldier.

She pulled herself to her feet with assistance from one of the Guards. "No, we are not good. Someone just yanked Kyra, the Traveler, through the portal."

At her words, the area went quiet, and a few people paled. "Who is in charge on this side?" asked Angie.

"I'll go get him," muttered someone who quickly took off down the path. It didn't take long for a familiar cat shape to approach.

"Brutis? This is what you've been doing?" asked Angie as he shifted into his large human form.

"It's good to see you," said Brutis. "What's going on?"

Angie recapped what had happened with Kyra, not that she really knew anything.

"Kyra vanishes right after Carter and Betha go running through a portal." said Brutis. "Has anyone gone through to see where it goes?"

Angie shook her head. "I mean, I tried to follow them from the Terra side but ended up here, and clearly they didn't. From what I understand, this portal should still go to Terra, we just don't know if it's still at the Nexus on that side. But I'm not exactly an expert here."

Brutis nodded at one of the guys, and he withdrew his sword before going through the portal. It only took him a few minutes to come back.

"That is not the Nexus."

A deep call like someone blowing on a horn sounded in the distance, and Angie turned in that direction. It wasn't coming from down the path, but off to the side where Betha had needed to go. That wasn't good.

"Brutis, what was the plan here?"

"Just to keep the path open. No hunting, no offense, just keep it clear of demons trying to cross. Shit!" he said in frustration.

Angie took a deep breath, thinking over the situation.

Betha was gone, and now so was Kyra. Where did they go? "I know of a safe campsite, but it is down the trail, almost five hours of slow walking. Faster if we hustle. Or we can defend this location if you guys think we have enough Guards. Thoughts?"

Some of the Guards surrounding her were shifters, but most were elves and trolls. It wasn't a huge group, fifteen or so, plus her and Brutis.

"We can't let them go through the portal, and we can't ambush them on the other side because once it moves back, we'll be stuck." said one of the other Guards, a veteran by the look of him. Between the scar on one side of his face and how he confidently stood, it was clear this situation didn't phase him.

"Did you recognize the other side?" Brutis asked the Guard who had scouted the portal.

"Just some forest. Lots of evergreen," the shifter replied. "It wasn't pack land, I know that."

The horn sounded again, closer. Angie had learned about this in history class—the portal from the elves went to a forest north of the council lands. But where did the fey wilds originally go to? Angie tried to think.

"Remember, don't attack first. Everyone pull back into a defensive formation. Pack, relay orders."

Brutis gave her a nod and shifted back into his large cat form. It took him longer than she thought was normal. Angie pulled off the pants she had on, along with her T-shirt. She folded them, and one of the guys grabbed them.

"*Here we go,*" she thought to herself.

Angie shifted into her wolf form. Then she headed for

the underbrush. The sun was heading closer to the horizon, and shadows dotted the path. They seemed to reach out to her, wanting her to vanish into them. Yet, she resisted. Last time, she had been fine, though she had only stayed in the shadow realm for a single heartbeat. This time she would be as well—she had to be. The Guard behind her spread out, and she noticed Brutis climbed a tree to hide in the branches.

Deep inside, she knew she would vanish if needed to save these guys. Maybe her heart was too big, but they were here enforcing the treaty terms. The portal must be open for trade and to keep her world safe. They were her people, at least for now, and together, they would hold. They had to.

CHAPTER
EIGHTEEN

Genessa marched up to the portal which began to swirl in a deep blue color. Betha took a step back, bumping into Carter. Heat and silver light suddenly radiated off of Genessa, twisting from her body. The sky darkened to the same deep blue as the portal. Bright white stars shimmered in the sky, twinkling in and out.

"What's going on?" asked Carter.

"No freaking idea," replied Betha under her breath.

"Where are you, Kyra?" muttered Genessa, staring into the portal.

Betha wasn't sure what the older woman could see since the portal was so dark. "She should be at the Nexus. She's normally there," said Betha.

"Found her," grunted Genessa. Then she reached into the portal and yanked. Hard.

Kyra stumbled across the threshold, along with Grandpappy, whose arms were around her waist.

"What did you do?" asked Betha. Kyra couldn't be

here. She couldn't travel through portals—that's what she'd said.

"Grammie?" asked Kyra, tangled up with Grandpappy and clearly in some level of shock. Her eyes were wide open, her skin pale. Dark circles were beneath her hazel eyes. The two of them untangled themselves and slowly climbed to their feet. Kyra stared at Genessa. "You're dead...aren't you?"

"Not dead, dear." Genessa held out her arms, inviting a hug. "I bonded with a node."

Kyra wrapped her arms around her grandmother. Her head fell onto Genessa's shoulder, and she shook. "You are stretching yourself too much, my dear. Your energy levels are far too low," the older woman said, stroking Kyra's hair.

"I...I..."

"She was saving Terra from the demons," answered Grandpappy. His eyes flicked over to Betha's, and he gave her a nod. "We were just asking Angie about where you had gotten off to, young lady."

"Well," Betha motioned around them, "we are here at Genessa's node."

Carter said, "What about the Nexus?"

Kyra pulled away from Genessa. "Oh, goddess! I shouldn't be here. The Nexus will fail."

"Kyra, this Nexus nonsense has to end. You can't hold that many portals forever," said Genessa. "This is fixable, though."

"I need to go back," whispered Kyra. "I have no choice."

"You need to find Guardians for those portals! You

can't hold them yourself much longer. Look how drained you are. You will fade away!"

Kyra snapped out of her panic and turned back toward Genessa. "Angie said something about Guardians as well. They are children's stories! They can't really exist."

Betha wasn't sure whether to speak up or stay quiet next to Carter. Grandpappy took a step closer to the two of them as if seeking shelter from this emotional storm.

"They aren't children's stories, and if you had stuck around instead of running away, you would have learned that." Genessa pushed Kyra away, holding her at arm's length and looking into her eyes. "You should have come back!"

"I couldn't. A seer warned me the whole branch would fall if I did!" exclaimed Kyra.

"She lied!" Genessa screeched. "A branch never depends on one Traveler. Never! You would have known if you had only trusted me."

Kyra stumbled backward as if she had been struck. "Seers don't lie. They can't." Her face had gone white, and she shook her head as though to deny what Genessa had said.

"And who told you that, dear?" asked Genessa. "I bet it was that same seer, wasn't it? But Andrea did lie, about that and about much else, I'm sure."

Betha stepped forward, drawing Kyra's attention. "Andrea was working with the demons. We were captured, and she tried to take the knife from me."

Grandpappy had to dart forward and catch Kyra before she hit the ground. Her knees just crumbled.

"That's not possible. It can't be, Andrea warned us of so many things. Without her, the council would have failed," he said while Kyra regained her feet.

"Just because she helped you out didn't mean it wasn't for her own reasons," answered Genessa. "Andrea was banished from our home and forbidden from contacting any Travelers. You, Kyra, were too young to know about it. You were expected to trust your family and come finish your lessons. If you had, you would have been told. But no, you knew better." The glint of steel in Genessa's eyes made it clear that Kyra could not shift her responsibility so easily.

"Why did she do this?" asked Kyra in a soft, defeated voice.

"To get the knife and find a way to the heart," answered Genessa. "That's why she was banished in the first place."

"How do you even know this?" Kyra asked.

"If you don't believe me, we can ask her directly," Genessa replied.

Betha's hand grabbed Carter's. Andrea was dead. She hadn't made it through the portal. *"Isn't she dead?"* asked Betha through their bond.

"She vanished with you. There wasn't a body," replied Carter.

"Come. It is time to finish this," said Genessa. "Do the two of you want to go on your way?" She glanced at Betha and then at Carter.

"I..." Betha stammered, not sure what to say.

"We need to see this," answered Carter. "We need to find out what is going on. She betrayed us, too."

Genessa nodded and walked down the path through the rose bushes.

Betha glanced at Grandpappy and Kyra. They both were pale, but at least Grandpappy was upright. Kyra was being held up by him and was no longer hanging limply. "Are you two okay?" Betha asked.

"No," answered Grandpappy. "Andrea's seer visions determined much on Terra for centuries. Some of the things we survived seemed impossible without her. If she was working for herself, though...I just don't know what to think."

"James, I'm sorry," said Kyra, pain clear in her voice.

"Not now, Kyra. We need to see this through," growled Grandpappy, clearly angry at how Andrea had used them all. He scooped her up into his arms and started down the trail.

"But, the Nexus," said Kyra.

"They can do without us for a time. This is more important," he replied.

Carter nudged Betha in the side. "Come on," he said, trailing the group.

Betha nodded and followed him, reaching forward and taking his hand. She glanced back at the portal, which had become solid stone. The sky was still a deep dark blue color with stars, and the smell of roses filled the air. Yet, something was different. The power that had been rolling off Genessa when she was looking for Kyra was gone.

When the path opened back up, it wasn't the same field. Instead, a giant boulder stood in the middle. Genessa stood close to the boulder, and Kyra was back on her feet, standing with Grandpappy's arm around her waist, but standing on her own.

KYRA DIDN'T KNOW what to do. James set her down on her feet and she forced herself to stand straighter. If Andrea had lied to them, she didn't know how to even process that. So much she had done, from forming the council to having the council sign treaties with different worlds, had been based on Andrea's advice. Her supposedly infallible, honest advice. Just how much had she thrown everything off?

"Are you ready for this?" asked Genessa.

Kyra nodded and moved closer to James. He had been her rock for so long.

Genessa tapped the boulder next to her. The spot seemed to shimmer, then the rock slowly vanished from that point like a wave going out to sea. Betha gasped. This type of magic was limited to nodes, and only available to the one bonded to it. Here her grandmother was, bonded with the node closest to the Nexus. All this time, she had been right here. Yet, Kyra hadn't even tried to find out what had happened to her. But she had been so sure. Andrea had been so confident that her grandmother had died and joined with the leylines. How could Kyra have known?

Inside the stone, Andrea was tied to a chair. Her shoulder was bandaged up, and she looked like crap. Her clothing was torn, and she was dirty. Her eyes snapped open, landing on Kyra.

"Kyra, get me out of here! She's crazy!" Andrea struggled in the bonds, but the chair didn't move.

Kyra resisted the urge to leap into action. She had jumped whenever Andrea had spoken for so long, it was hard to hold her ground. But she knew Genessa wouldn't lie to her— not here, not now. She probably never had, and that was the scariest thought.

Genessa approached the chair, drawing Andrea's attention. "Get away from me, heretic!" yelled the bound seer.

"You know better," said Genessa. She reached into her pocket and drew out a golden metal rod flattened on one end like a brand. She touched it to Andrea's forehead, and a mark appeared underneath. "Now, let's hear the truth. Were you banned from any contact with Travelers?"

Andrea tried to keep her lips sealed but couldn't resist answering. "Yes."

"Who is that?" asked Genessa while pointing to Kyra.

"Kyra. A Traveler."

"You became friends with Kyra even though you were banned from contact with Travelers. Is this correct?"

"Yes." Each answer was being wrenched from Andrea's lips by the magic in the rod. Clearly, she wouldn't have answered otherwise.

"What were you hoping to gain from breaking the banishment and becoming friends with her?" asked Genessa.

"I wanted the knife! It was going to show up on Terra at some point. I just needed to be patient."

"The magic is working. What do you two want to know?" Genessa asked Kyra.

Kyra cleared her throat. "What would the knife help you accomplish?"

"I could get to the heart. The heart is everything."

The heart wasn't everything. Friends and family were everything. And Kyra had given up her blood family to help the family she had found on Terra. All because this traitor advised her to. No one was allowed to go to the heart. Not anymore. It used to be their home a long time ago. Then a Traveler turned their back on everything, and all were banished. This deceitful creature couldn't ever be allowed to go there even if she somehow could find a way.

"How did you help the demons?" asked Kyra.

Andrea growled, clearly resisting, before her lips finally parted. "I told the king secrets he shouldn't know about how to increase his power, but he wouldn't trade the knife. Then I influenced the prince to take over Terra."

She really had done it. All of those people were dead just so she could try to get her hands on one of the knives. How could she?

"The princess needed the Traveler, so I made sure she could be captured. I was so close!" Andrea's voice rose as she spoke.

"Why did you encourage my wife to leave Terra?" asked James.

"She was getting in the way. She knew something was off with me. The shadowed ones can feel the balance. I needed to get rid of her."

Kyra just stood there in shock as Carter dashed forward, stopping James from doing anything he would regret. Andrea really had done all of this. Encouraged her to create the council, stopped her from leaving Terra, and locked her into forming the Nexus. They had walked right into the trap because she was a seer. Seers always worked for the greater good. They had to, or really bad things happened to them. The fates did not respond kindly to those who twisted the powers of fate the wrong way.

"James," whispered Kyra.

Fur had sprouted along his face, and his teeth had gotten longer. He had suffered so much all for a greater good that was a lie.

"Grandpappy?" asked Betha in a small voice.

Betha's voice seemed to reach the beast inside of him, and he pushed Carter off before turning his back on the woman in the chair.

Kyra didn't know what to do. Her gaze rose to find Grammie staring at her. Who knew what was happening on Terra or with the worlds it was connected to via the nexus? If Genessa was right, she could fix it. She had to. Yet, what else did they need to know?

"Did you know about me and my mother?" asked Betha before Kyra could gather her thoughts.

"Not until you showed up at St. Luna's. You were blocked from my visions. I knew someone important was coming, but some other seer protected you." Hate spilled out of Andrea's mouth. "Whoever they are, they kept trying to fix things. Change them and move the path I was working with. Redirect my efforts."

"What about my father?" added Betha.

"No idea."

Kyra glanced at Betha quickly, wondering why she was asking about her father. But now was not the time. An important question came to mind. "Why were you banished and forbidden from contacting Travelers?" asked Kyra.

Genessa jerked as Kyra spoke. Her eyes shut, and Kyra braced herself for what was to come.

"My sister was the Seen, and all involved were banished! All who dared to hope there was a different way to be. No longer tied to the whims of the Tree. Free to make our own choices and be our own people! But no, we were shoved out into the universe." Spittle sprayed from her lips. "Left to wander without power. Betrayed by our people!"

Genessa stepped forward and snapped her fingers. "Enough!" The rod glowed in her fingers, and Andrea's mouth snapped shut. "Have you heard enough?" Genessa asked the others.

Kyra nodded and jumped as James wrapped an arm around her. His voice was deep as he said, "We heard what we needed to."

Genessa stepped backward, and the rock that had been there before slowly formed back into place.

"You can't leave me here!" screamed the trapped woman.

Her voice was finally cut off as the stone slowly filled in. Kyra shuddered and closed her eyes for a moment. This was not what she thought today was going to bring.

"The Nexus needs Guardians." Her voice was quiet,

but James tightened his arm around her. She needed to find a way to fix the Nexus without it draining her life away. She had been so sure in her belief in Andrea, she hadn't even questioned it. "I believe that now. How do I do that?"

"I could ask the gargoyles, but..." started Betha. Kyra snapped her eyes over to the young Traveler. She was biting her lip and looking at Carter. They had to be having a conversation. "...stopping the demons is more important. And they only recently remembered their purpose. I can't ask this of them too," Betha finished.

Genessa cut in, "This isn't for the gargoyles to do. You have your mission, Betha, and a plan for it. You need to focus on the hells. Kyra needs to focus on the Nexus. This is something she created, and she needs to be the one to finish it."

"How, Grammie? How do I find Guardians for the Nexus? Betha says gargoyles can do it, but you say it's not for them to do. How can I do this without them?"

"I will explain. You are going to need to start with those that you bound yourself with to anchor the peace. It is time they paid their dues."

Kyra's fingers tighten around James' arm. Her nails slightly digging in. He knew who she was anchored to. Not all were her choices, and not all had been worthy, but she hadn't forced anyone to do anything they hadn't wanted to. Now she would have to do just that.

"Come Betha, Carter—it is time you were on your way. Kyra has much to do yet, as do you. Time you all got started," said Genessa. She walked back toward the portal of stone.

CHAPTER
NINETEEN

Betha followed Genessa down the path, avoiding eye contact with Kyra. The older Traveler was white as a sheet, and Grandpappy looked just as tormented. Betha had thought his wife had died, not that she had left Terra. She certainly hadn't known it was Andrea's fault. She guessed Kyra and Grandpappy had a lot of reasons to look upset.

Still, it wasn't the time to ask. They had more pressing matters. The demons needed to be stopped and she needed to do it. Poor Kyra—she was going to need to bond her Anchors to the portals. Everything in Betha hoped that Grandpappy wasn't going to be one of them. He was the only Anchor they had seen with Kyra. The rest of them could pay the price, but Grandpappy was family.

"What's going to happen to Andrea now?" asked Betha. She wasn't sure what the stone prison was about, but usually when someone broke laws, there were consequences. She hoped there would be consequences. Andrea had caused a lot of pain.

Genessa let a sigh escape. "The crime she committed is worth her life. We don't deal lightly with the banished."

"So she will die," said Betha, her voice hollow.

"Not yet, unfortunately. I will keep her hidden away for now. She spoke of things that I thought were done with, and I want to check in with some other nodes first. Just to make sure this isn't a bigger problem, you understand. For now, Betha, you need to focus on the hells. Already you have stabilized many of the worlds this node connects to. This is very important work."

"The Guardian that faded had said that before he vanished. He said that tears were starting to heal on their own."

Betha studied the portal in front of her. It was somehow different from other portals, but she couldn't explain it. It felt like it *was* the in-between—a part of it, not just a portal between worlds. Maybe it wasn't a portal at all. The sky overhead was still dark blue.

"They will if the leylines are healthy enough and if nearby portals are guarded. There aren't enough Travelers to heal every tear. It's like an ecosystem—when things are in balance, we don't have much to do. It's when things get off, like with the demons, that we are needed."

"Once Betha takes care of the demons, this ecosystem will be in a better place?" asked Carter.

"Exactly. The more portals that are guarded, the more balanced the powers in the worlds, the more that it will take care of itself. You have a good plan. It should succeed." Genessa gave both of them a smile. The portal glowed with a bright white light. "This will take you to Sky World. You might be able to use the knife to get closer to the Sky Stone. It is connected like a portal, but I can't reach it directly from here. It has been too long since I was there."

Betha nodded. She was going to try to use the knife, especially if it could shave a few days off their trip. "Thank you for the info and the help. I feel like I might actually have fewer questions than when I got here, which is definitely a change for the better."

"Of course. I'm sorry you needed to witness that, but I wasn't going to hide it. May the fates be with you. And remember, I'm here when you are ready to learn more, when the worlds are more in balance."

Betha grabbed Carter's hand. His face had a very serious look on it. She focused on Sky World. The color of the sky, how the trees looked, and how everything smelled. The crisp air with hints of pine. A picture of little Jadon came to mind. She was going to see her friends again. Then she stepped through the portal, and they were inundated with rain.

"Welcome back, Traveler," whispered Magson. They both quickly darted under the trees to find some relief from the downpour.

"We did it!" said Betha, pumping her fist in excitement. She felt like she was actually getting a handle on her abilities with Genessa's help, and that was exciting.

The clearing was the one below Rock Camp. They had made it to the gargoyle's home world. The pine trees blocked most of the rain, but it was not exactly an ideal weather day. All she needed to do was use the knife to get them to the Sky Stone. It would be dry in the building at least, and hopefully Talli or Sir Samson would be nearby.

"Back on Sky World," said Carter. "It's only been a few days, but it feels like it has been longer."

"I don't remember if time goes by quicker here or slower. I do remember the days themselves are longer." It was hard to judge the speed of time after you traveled through several worlds to get there.

Betha summoned the knife to her hand and took a deep breath. She wasn't sure how to do this. Last time, she had stabbed out and just concentrated on fleeing. This time, she had a destination in mind. But even Genessa hadn't been sure it was doable. No way to know unless she tried.

"Let me hold on tight first," muttered Carter. He moved behind her and wrapped his arms around her midsection. She paused, enjoying the moment, and leaned her head back against his chest.

"You got this," whispered Carter into her hair. Betha tried not to think about the fact that they had been traveling for the last several days and her hair was filthy. Instead, she pictured the Sky Stone inside her head.

"We need to go to the Sky Stone." Betha flooded her hand with power down into the knife. Her mark glowed like the moon, and the knife pulsed. Then they were gone.

Her feet weren't touching anything as they appeared. Gravity took over, and Betha crashed to her knees onto the hard stone. Pain flared up on contact, and everything else felt like jelly. Carter rolled to one side so as not to crush her.

A hoarse yell followed by a grunt came from that side.

The knife vanished as she accidentally let go, trying to catch herself before the rest of her hit the ground. The edges of her sight started to go black. Her hand landed on the Sky Stone, and the room flared a bright white. Energy flowed into her as a map rolled across the room.

The darkness receded and she steadied.

"Betha?"

Betha blinked at the sound and let go of the Stone. They were here. Multiple gargoyles stood in the doorway staring at them. Sir Samson stepped forward. He wasn't looking at her though. His gaze was to one side, filled with horror.

"Garson! What did you do?" asked Sir Samson. He darted forward, and Betha turned. Her angel was slumped to one side, blood dripping from his head. A knife stuck out of his back. A gargoyle with a terrified expression knelt next to him, shaking.

"I didn't mean to! It was so sudden," chanted the gargoyle as he rocked back and forth. Scabs covered his body, along with scars of small two-inch lines.

"Carter!" Her voice was a harsh, pained whisper. She reached out through the bond, and he was still there. Betha crawled next to him as Sir Samson checked to see if he was still breathing.

"How did you get here?" asked the gargoyle.

"We traveled," replied Betha.

"I think he hit his head on the stone when you both fell. Someone fetch Nalli! Quickly!" he said with authority.

Betha didn't know what to do. She wasn't a healer. In fact, the only one she knew who wasn't an angel was back on Terra now. More blood flowed from the wound, and Sir Samson applied pressure with a cloth to it while leaving the knife alone.

"Oh, fates, is he going to be okay?" Panic rose inside of her, but she could feel him within the bond. Plus, he did heal quickly. Betha pushed the panic away and tried to take a deep breath. She grabbed his hand, holding on tight. Yet, something was wrong with the bond. He was there, but faded, and Betha fought to keep the rising panic under control.

"We can't remove the knife until Nalli gets here," muttered Sir Samson. "He will be okay."

"Move! Clear this space!" came from the doorway. Nalli rushed inside, taking in the scene.

"Betha?" Her footsteps slowed, then she shook it off. "What happened?"

"He hit his head when we appeared too high in the air," Betha replied. At least that's what she thought had happened. Her feet hadn't been touching the ground, then she hit her knees. Which didn't hurt anymore. Because she had touched the stone.

"And then Garson panicked and stabbed him," finished Sir Samson.

Nalli noticed the knife and dove to her knees. "I don't know angel anatomy, but that is not a good spot."

The bond between the two of them shook, and Betha

panicked. "He needs to touch the stone." She grabbed his hand and nudged the edge of it to the rock. Nothing happened. "Why isn't it working!"

Nalli's hands shook as she touched the hilt of the knife. "Betha, breathe. I need information. He might bleed out when we remove it. How quickly does his healing factor work?"

"I don't know, it just works." He needed to heal like Eric could heal. He needed more power. Betha scrambled free of Carter and snagged the archangel feather from her boot. It was then she noticed how much Carter was bleeding. The feather sparkled in the light, and she gripped it tightly. It cut into her fingertips as she pressed it into his hand. "You need to heal him! Give the power to him!"

Angel fire flickered from the contact for a split second, then the scent of burning flesh filled the room. Carter's body jerked, and all of the gargoyles recoiled. The knife was pushed out of his back and hit the stone floor. The feather vanished from beneath her fingertips.

Carter gasped for breath, and his eyes fluttered. His chest kept moving. The bond inside her head blazed.

"Let's get him to the healer's space next door," said Nalli. Betha let her fingers drop from his. Sir Samson pulled Carter up in his arms with a grunt and marched out of the room. Nalli quickly followed. Betha pulled herself up but paused.

"I didn't mean to," said Garson in a small voice.

Betha's gaze landed on the still-shaking gargoyle. She took a step in his direction.

"Forgive me!" His voice came out as a croak as another gargoyle approached.

"Accidents happen," said Betha.

"Garson, it's okay." The second gargoyle had his empty hands raised and approached Garson carefully.

"No, it's not. I hurt my sister and now I hurt our friends! The ones who saved us. I'm not safe! They broke me!" Garson darted forward and grabbed the knife. Both Betha and the other gargoyle stepped back. "The demons broke me. Take me, take me as tribute! I beg you!" He sliced deeply into his hand and slapped it onto the stone. Bright light washed over the room, and he was gone. His bloody handprint remained on the white surface of the stone.

"Garson," whispered the gargoyle. Tears rolled down his face, and Betha stepped toward him.

"I...I am so sorry," she managed.

"They tortured him for weeks. We found him in a demon camp and brought him here. We hoped the stone could fix his mind." The gargoyle wrapped his arms around himself. "I'll have someone clean the room up."

Betha fled, her thoughts racing. She followed her connection to Carter, heading to the healer's space where he was. She could feel him, yet she couldn't touch his mind. It was wrapped in white light that reminded her of angel fire. This was the first time that she couldn't connect with him even though he was close. Well, the first time since he'd manifested, and then she'd been around her other Anchors. Now there was no one else, just Carter, and he was hurt. She hadn't felt this alone in a long time, since before she bonded with Angie.

Betha tried to calm her heart rate but gave up and kept moving. He had to be all right. The connection led her to a nearby open doorway. The rain must have stopped here, but everything was still wet. The room had several beds set up and a small fire going in the center. Carter lay on one of the beds with Sir Samson standing nearby.

Nalli pulled a bowl of hot water away from the coals and removed the cloth on Carter's head. "Well, the wound has stopped bleeding." She used the water to clean out the cut. Betha sat down on the edge of the bed. "I'll get this bandaged up and try to get him to wake up. Hopefully, he heals quickly," said Nalli.

"I...we all heal quickly but I don't know how to measure it." Betha's voice quavered with her fear, but she tried to steady it. "I don't know what the feather did. Garson vanished into the Sky Stone."

Sir Samson leaned against a wall with his eyes closed. "Why are you here now?"

Betha shook her head with a frown, thankful for the distraction. "We know where the demon king is, and we can trap him if gargoyles are willing to bond with portals. Like Derrik, without the call. I was hoping to stop this once and for all with the help of your people."

"That must have been a hard decision," his voice was soft.

"At this point, it has to stop. The demons are trying to kill the king as well, but they can't because of his power. I thought if we could trap him, it might be good enough." Betha's voice broke. She shouldn't have brought him. Why did she wait to go through the portal?

Then she would have been the only one at Genessa's, and now here. And Carter wouldn't be unconscious on a bed in front of her.

"Then you are under a time crunch as well," observed Sir Samson.

All she could do was nod. Her eyes stayed on Carter in the bed. Nalli finished checking him over and slid a pillow under his head. She used a finger to open his eyes and she made a sigh. "I think he just needs to rest and, somehow, we need to get him to eat. The feather healed the physical wounds from the knife and the fall. I don't know what else it did to him but magical healing usually causes people to burn an enormous amount of energy." Nalli pulled a small pouch out and opened it under his nose. Betha reached out through the bond at the same time that he jerked. His eyelids fluttered and he jerked upright before lying back down.

"Carter?" asked Betha.

"It hurts."

"Carter, open your eyes," said Nalli.

"Can you open your eyes?"

"Can't, need sleep…" his thoughts trailed off as he fell into unconsciousness again.

"He said he couldn't, and I think he is sleeping. Or out cold," said Betha, still worried.

Nalli's eyes drew together, and she glanced at Sir Samson. "Do you think one of the healers would come here?"

"Some of the angels are helping the trolls hunt down the remaining demons, but many have left already. I can send a messenger once they return, but it will take a few days for them to find anyone. We don't know if any healers are still here," replied Sir Samson.

"What would you normally do?" asked Betha.

Nalli pressed her lips together before answering. "If he just needed rest to recover with his quick healing, I would leave him be. But if his head were still injured after he'd rested, I would have him touch the stone. Head injuries, when they can't stay awake, are bad. I don't know if it is the same for angels."

Betha closed her eyes and took another deep breath. They needed gargoyles to stop the king. Carter would heal because of his angelic blood. He needed time, that was all. It would have to be.

"I mean, their wings will grow back. Or at least Parian said his would once he got back to the heavens. I think we just need to give him a few days." Betha forced her voice to be hopeful. Maybe she could even make herself believe it.

"The messenger should be back tomorrow, that will give him time," said Sir Samson. "We should let him rest."

Betha nodded and stood. She pressed down the panic as deep as she could. She leaned over and kissed his cheek, then headed out the door. He would have to be okay, but she couldn't fix him. She would finish what they'd started. That, she could do.

IT HURT. His bones ached, along with the fire in his chest. He knew something had happened. The dying part hadn't hurt. Everything had started to go dark and quiet. It had been peaceful. Then he had been hit with a fire-ball, and it shook him. The ball of angel fire inside his chest rose up to meet and challenge it. The two forces met and almost seemed to fight. One, the bright golden light, the other, more silver and cold.

His own bright ball of angel fire sputtered, and he grasped it with everything he had. He knew it must not go out. Foreboding filled his thoughts as he focused on the ball, on his angel fire. It kept sputtering, and Carter panicked. The bonds in the back of his mind flickered, and he latched onto the one the same color as his angel fire. Thoughts of Eric filled his mind, and he pulled. Energy rushed into him, and tendrils grew from the ball. Instead of attacking, they wrapped around the cold silver light, yanking it inside itself. It shook hard, then flared. The connection with his brother snapped. His ball grew and expanded in his chest in strange ways. Brighter, stronger, and more volatile. Yet, strength radiated out from it, filling his limbs. Whatever the cold ball had been, it was his now. And he had no idea what that meant.

~

THE BOND FLICKERED in the back of Eric's mind, pulling him from a deep sleep.

"Carter? Betha?" His voice called out in the darkness of the room, but also across the bonds he shared with both of them. It had been too long since he had felt those connections.

The hair on the back of his neck stood up. Something was wrong. Carter kept coming to mind. He wiped the sleep from his eyes and turned on the light. Right now, he was in Haven, and everything in him said he needed to get back to the Nexus. Something was wrong with Carter. Power flared in his chest and, for a moment, he could feel his brother in the room with him. He needed help. Eric reached out with the bond they shared. "Carter! Take it, take what you need!"

His chest hurt, and his body trembled. Something happened, and Carter was gone. It took several moments for him to stop shaking. The blanket slid off of him, and he quickly dressed in the soft light. His father was still here, and there was too much going on, but he needed answers.

Angie was at the Nexus, which reduced his fear. He knew Kellion was there too. Eric hadn't wanted to leave the Nexus at all, but Kellion had promised to stay in the city as long as it took for them to come back. It hadn't made his father happy, but keeping Eric close had been more important.

It didn't take long for him to get dressed, but even so, just as he was going to head out to the balcony to start the very long flight, Angie vanished. Just like that, she was gone. "What?" he said under his breath. This didn't make any sense, but he knew they had been there. Something was going on. With a sigh he pulled out his phone, dialing Kellion. Hopefully, he had some answers.

CHAPTER
TWENTY

The sky was clearing up, and patches of blue were overhead instead of the pouring rain. Betha leaned against the damp stone ledge surrounding the drop-off. This was not going to plan.

"Did the gargoyles who left make it?" asked Sir Samson.

"Most. Only a few couldn't make it across the Fey Wilds. More portals are guarded. Balin made it." She turned toward him. "We spoke to the old Guardian, and Balin bonded with the portal." Betha shook her head. "I was hoping to be able to travel with them to portals to block the king so they were out of danger, but..."

"You both made it here. The landing was rough. It always takes practice to land on your feet."

"You would know about that," said Betha with a chuckle.

"It's one of the first things we teach since once you go up, you have to come down. How are your knees?" asked Sir Samson with a slight smile.

Betha had forgotten she had hit them. "Fine. When I touched the stone, it filled me with energy. I think it healed them."

"At least you don't need to worry about the call."

"Was that a joke?"

"I tried," said Sir Samson ruefully. "How bad is it out there?"

"The demons are causing trouble all over the Fey Wilds, which we didn't know there were rules for. Though the rules seem to be almost unimportant since the demons ignore them."

"Rules? What rules?" asked the gargoyle.

"For using the trading route," replied Betha.

"We have flown through the Fey Wilds without problems before, but we don't have any rules. The angels might. We haven't needed them, though." Sir Samson cocked his head as though the idea of rules for traveling through the fey lands was an odd concept.

"Well, the demons are breaking all the rules and attacking people," said Betha.

"I wouldn't want to upset the fey lords. We have old stories we tell around the fire, but only for the grown ones. The little bats must be in bed. Otherwise, they might not sleep," he replied. "They are not pleasant stories—the ones where the fey lords are upset. Though, they seem to always be fair. Just not pleasant when upset."

Betha could only imagine the nightmares she would have had when she was a kid from stories about the fey lords. Whatever Angie had been worried about when they had been on the road to the portal to Terra had been bad enough, and Betha hadn't even seen or felt it. Her best friend had been shaken, and Angie was one of the bravest people she had ever known. All she knew was that she would follow the rules now that she understood them.

"Do you think some gargoyles will volunteer?" asked Betha.

Sir Samson gave a small shrug, his wings moving in the air. "We lost many from the demons, but you are here and helped our people get back on track. How many do you need?"

Betha wished she had a better answer, but she only had a guess. "I think five. I can find out and give you a solid number. I need to go visit the stone, though."

His wings relaxed. "Five isn't bad. We have had a few more be called, but not many more. The elders were concerned that all would be called, given that we haven't held up our end of the bargain for so long. It was one of the arguments against reopening the stone after the accursed one blocked it off. We were worried that there would be...retribution."

Given how many people they had lost in the battles with the demons, Betha understood the concern. It would take them a long time to rebuild. Many villages had been completely wiped out.

"The more portals that are guarded, the easier the leylines and tears can heal on their own. I have healed much by myself, and I plan to do more. That will help as well. Right now, though, the biggest concern is the demons. If they stop upsetting the balance and increasing the damage, we can start to fix it. I don't think it needs to happen all at once."

"Just this one time."

"To trap the demon king."

"Why doesn't someone kill him?" asked Sir Samson

"Someone would replace him," interrupted Talli, coming up from behind. "They will always have a leader. Trapping him forces them to pause. It is a good idea."

Betha smiled at the elder as she joined them. "The princess and I made a deal. If I can trap him, she can take over and recall all of the demons she can reach."

Talli studied her. "Is that wise?" asked the elder, her concern evident by the care with which she kept her face expressionless.

"I don't trust her, but it is still a good plan. Even if she doesn't recall all of the other demons, if he's trapped, then so is she. Healing the tears and guarding the portals solves the biggest problems either way."

"Another group of survivors came in from the plains to see if their children were here. It was a happy moment. We couldn't have survived without you. You will get your volunteers, I'm not worried. The fates are on your side," said Talli as she turned to lean against the wall with the two of them. They stared into the distance in silence.

Angie could feel her heart pounding. The horn sounded again in the distance, but she didn't know what it meant. Deep breaths were needed. Focus was going to be key in this fight. They had nowhere to run to that was within reach, especially for the non-shifters.

The bond in the back of her mind crackled.

"*Betha?*"

She was there just for a moment, but then she was gone. A feeling about Carter washed over her, but she shook it off. It was strange. Hopefully, her friend was portal hopping and not anywhere near this battlefield. While Betha could take care of herself, they both had come to the conclusion that this wasn't the place for her. Or for Angie. While she was good at fighting, she didn't want it anymore. It wore her down after everything was over and she was trying to sleep. Yet adrenaline filled her now. There were people here to protect.

The shadows were right there. Not yet. Only if she needed to.

The smell of many demons washed over her. It was the same as when she had darted to the portal to get to Terra. She ran her nose over the back of one of her paws since she couldn't stand still. They were getting close enough that she could hear them in the underbrush.

Must not strike first. Must not strike first.

A multi-winged creature no bigger than a small bird flew frantically away from the marching demons. Angie assumed it was one of the fey given its brightly colored wings similar to those of a butterfly. Wings protruded from the fey's back, and much smaller ones that didn't seem to move as much sat on either side of its head. Big brown eyes and a small mouth took up the bulk of its face. Fur covered its body, and instead of feet, it had claws like a bird. It headed directly toward the portal in panic, but froze in front of the Guards, flapping its wings to hover above the ground.

One of the soldiers called out to it. "We are protecting the portal. We won't harm you. The portal isn't heading to the Nexus right now, though." The creature nodded, then darted to the rear of the group. It didn't cross the portal but instead hung nearby. The soldier's voice was soft, but Angie could hear it. "If things are going south, make sure you flee, little one."

Things were not going to go south. It took everything to not howl a war song at the incoming demons. She could now see them marching through the trees. It was the same group as before—black leather armor, swords, and wicked claws. Red eyes glowed beneath black horns. They all looked of similar build with broad shoulders, and all stood tall. Growls came from behind the demon soldiers, and they stopped.

A bigger demon strode forward with a bright red helmet and jagged horns that rose on either side of his head. He had to be at least seven feet tall. He growled something, and dark figures close to the ground moved to the front. Angie didn't flinch at the sight of the hellhounds. Doglike creatures with spikes running down their spines, teeth too big for their mouths, and quick bursts of fire breath—they were a familiar foe. They were smaller than her, but quick.

The leader raised his sword, and the hounds howled. Everything went silent. At least five hounds darted toward the edge of the trees and the Guards behind Angie. They broke into the sunlight, but still Angie did not move. The hounds were not her concern. The leader was. She assumed he was a lieutenant given his ornate helmet. If you cut the head off of a snake, it usually died. The demons needed hierarchy—that much she had figured out. Without the orders of a truly powerful lieutenant, they might have a shot.

Shouts, screams, and the sounds of fighting rose behind her, but none of the hounds had turned her way. The lieutenant waited a moment longer, then pointed his sword toward the group. The rest of the soldiers charged.

Just wait.

The soldiers rushed by the towering commander, and he just stood there. Still in the back. Did he plan to stay out of the action?

Not if Angie had anything to say about it.

She slipped into the shadow plane. Everything softened like it normally did. There was no pain; this was her place again.

The lieutenant hid in the shadows under the trees. She moved to circle behind him. His armor covered him very well, including his full helmet. Angie circled to find a good spot to attack. Her eyes landed on the back of his neck. The helmet didn't cover it all of the way. That would be her target.

Then she moved.

Angie flashed to the real world just long enough to snag her teeth in the back of his neck and use her weight to drag him down. Blood flooded her mouth, and it stung. He rolled away, and she had to let go. His helmet went flying. Angie dashed back to the shadow plane and coughed up what was in her mouth. Whatever he was, it was horrid.

After shaking her head, she focused back on the demon. His bright red eyes flicked about, going from tree to tree. The lieutenant had black hair, and his horns were gone. She realized they were attached to the helmet. He almost looked human if you took away the extra height, glowing eyes, and talons. Not to mention his burning blood that was most definitely not human.

He turned in a circle, completely distracted, trying to locate what had attacked him. Blood ran down the back of his armor, but she watched the wound start to close up. That was not good. Still, anything that bleeds can bleed to death. It was a lesson all shifters learned. While they could heal, they could be drained. This demon lieutenant would learn he could be drained, too.

She crouched down, waiting. Her eyes noticed that the backs of his knees weren't covered. The armor set was nice, but it didn't cover everything. It seemed designed primarily to defend attacks from the front. She assumed demons must fight head-on most of the time, given the shape of the armor. That was fine for her—frontal assault had never been her style.

A loud scream caused her to jerk, but she resisted looking back at the group fighting near the portal. This was her battle, this lieutenant. The demon smiled at the sound of battle. That was all she needed.

Angie darted out of the shadow plane enough to tear into the backs of his knees. Her claws hit bone and he fell forward. She dodged back into the shadow plane as his sword swung out. He tried to roll over to protect his back, but she didn't wait.

Her teeth dug into the back of his neck again, and she

yanked back and forth as hard as she could. This had to stop. Talons swiped at her face, and she let go at the sudden pain near her eye. The safety of the shadow plane was what she had. The demon tried to climb to his feet, but she had gotten his knees good. This time, she gagged harshly at the taste of the blood in her mouth.

The scratch on her face wasn't healing as quickly as she hoped. Then she realized her paws were tingling. Poison. His blood. Fuck.

He struggled on the ground, facing upward, but he didn't get up. Harsh breathing was still coming from him, and this was not over. Angie had to finish it. She darted out of the shadow plane, her claws raking over his eyes. A dark shape hit her side before she could shift into the darkness.

Angie hit some bushes and then shifted to the shadow plane. A hellhound paced around the fallen demon. She could still hear his breathing, which wasn't good. The longer in between damage, the longer this was going to take. Her paws still tingled, and she didn't know if that was a good thing or bad. Hopefully, her healing would take care of the poison. It wasn't like she had any other options.

The hellhound kept pacing because it couldn't sense her. Angie let out a deep breath. She needed to take out the hound and the demon. They didn't have time for this to stretch out and have more guards die. Angie ignored the hound and stared at the demon. His fingers reached out, searching for the handle of his sword. His face was a bloody mess, and blood still dripped from the wounds she had carved with her claws.

What to do. What to do.

Something rustled in the branches, and the hell-hound took off after it. Angie didn't wait. Rushing out of the shadows, she tore into his face again. Talons pushed at her, but this time she didn't let up. After an intense moment of struggle, his hands fell. Angie stumbled off of him and gagged again. It turned into dry heaving, but nothing came up.

Angie stumbled around on four paws and then shifted to her human form. Naked skin rolled out as her bones snapped, but she needed to get that taste out of her mouth. The sword he had been wielding was right there, so she grabbed it. Thankfully, Carter required all of them to learn to use swords. It was medium length and lighter than it should be. The blade had a twisted cross-guard, offering hand protection that looked almost like wings. Her focus switched to the sounds of fighting. The sword seemed way too pretty to be demon-made. Maybe this guy had found it or won it in some contest. Either way, she had it now.

Beyond the trees near the portal, several Guards still stood. Fallen demons and soldiers were on the ground. She could hear demons fleeing into the woods—they had done it. A dark shape moved near her, and she flinched, raising the sword. Cat eyes met hers, and the animal huffed as it tossed a dead hellhound her way.

"Brutis," said Angie, recognizing the great cat.

She stumbled out of the trees toward the Guards, but froze. A horned demon walked out of the trees, holding onto a Guard. She was elven, and her eyes stared ahead. Talons were wrapped around her throat, and blood was caked in her hair. Angie had no idea how she was still standing and noticed her eyes were having trouble focusing.

"Where is the Traveler?" growled the demon.

The Guard didn't move.

"Not here," answered Angie. She stood as confidently as she could while naked and holding a sword. "Drop the Guard and leave. This isn't going to end well for you."

"I want the Traveler!" His claws tightened around the elf Guard's neck.

Everything seemed to freeze. The red eyes on the demon grew wide, then he dropped the woman. Once she was free, he was yanked back into the trees. Angie caught a glimpse of vines dug into his back, and she swallowed hard. Then he was gone.

No one moved. No one dared to.

The small creature with wings that had hidden near the portal earlier rushed over to the elf on the ground. That spurred Angie into action, sending her darting over to the elf as fast as she could. Her bare feet pounded across the trail.

"Shit," she muttered. She checked the woman's pulse and found her heart still beating. "Let's move her near the portal," Angie said to the other Guards that were still standing.

The fey creature beat its colorful wings frantically and sprinkled dust on the elf's head wound. It squeaked in a high-pitched voice, pointing to the elf with its tiny hands.

"I don't know what you said, but I'm glad you are okay," answered Angie. A few of the Guards grabbed the elf and brought her near the portal. "Let's check the others, see if there are any other survivors."

Brutis was already sniffing various downed Guard when Angie turned back to the group. She needed to find her clothes and take a moment. Her fingers were shaking, but she held onto the sword.

They had survived. Or at least most of them had. This time. Now they just had to keep surviving until they figured out what to do next.

His power rolled through the land, picking off demons here and there. Any that moved outside of the treaty with the Nexus were simply taken care of. Any that tumbled out of tears that hadn't been there when he had gone to sleep were eaten. The forest would expand in the coming years from all of the food.

He had three portals of trade within his domain. One to the desert land, which the dwarves passed through from their home world, just like the gargoyles. A second led to the Nexus, where most of the travelers headed. And lastly, one to the small world of the lost goblins. This portal was covered by the treaty with the demon king. They were given safe passage to use the trade ways from it like all of the other races.

But the demons had taken that land and killed its people. It was now a crossroads. It was also where the bulk of the demons were gathering. They were smart, staying within the lines of treaties, even though those treaties were not theirs. They still bound him, and that meant they were in areas where he could not directly interfere. He would not break the treaties he had with other worlds, especially not with a shadow fen and Traveler nearby.

However, he could nudge some assistance toward the travelers currently honoring the treaties. A little helper—one of the fairies. Fairy dust could heal, and it would help those who were trying to hold the Nexus portal. And if the rose fey encouraged his cousins, the singing flowers, to get involved, then it would all be right on the edge of the line of what he could do. Plus, the singing flowers loved the shadow fen that sniffed them when no one was looking.

CHAPTER
TWENTY-ONE

Betha didn't know what to do. Carter wasn't awake yet, and Talli and Sir Samson had gone off to speak to the gargoyles. She had wandered outside to stare at the sky. The sky had cleared up from all of the rain, and not a cloud was in sight. The sun beat down on her and the heat felt good. She focused on a mountain in the far distance. She leaned against the balcony, just letting all of the anxiety rest. While she wanted to stay by Carter's side, she needed to do something productive. She needed to finish this. Slowly, she straightened when she was calm and headed to the doorway of the Sky Stone.

As she approached the room, the Sky Stone glimmered in the light, beckoning her to come inside. The room had been cleaned and it was empty. Gargoyles had been about earlier, but now this tier of the city was quiet. Betha shook her head and approached the white object. She carefully set both of her hands down on its surface. It surprised her to find the stone warm underneath her fingertips. Just like before, a map of the in-between rolled across her vision. Her senses expanded beyond the world she was on, and she could see the whole of this part of the great Tree of Life.

"Angie?" Betha sent, trying something.

She could feel her friend. The distance was farther than ever before, but Angie shone there in the distance. Maybe the Sky Stone could help her not be so alone.

"Betha? Is that you? Where are you?" Angie replied.

Betha nearly sobbed in relief. She hadn't realized how important it was to her to have her family nearby. Carter had been such a rock, but now with him unconscious, she was feeling very alone. But she wasn't. *"On Sky World. Getting gargoyles to trap the king. You are in the Fey Wilds?"* she replied after getting herself under control.

"Yeah, we're stuck. The Nexus is down—someone stole Kyra. Wait, how are you talking to me?"

"Uh, I wouldn't really say 'stole' Kyra, but yeah, she is with Genessa. As for talking to you, I don't really know how. Somehow it works, though, using the Sky Stone."

Betha quickly explained what had happened in Genessa's node, along with Carter hitting his head and being stabbed. Just talking it out with Angie made her feel better. She knew she wasn't alone, and that she could do this. And it helped her believe Carter would be okay.

"That is really bad luck, but he should be fine in a few days," Angie said.

"I don't know if we have a few days. The king should be in the fifth hell. I need to stop him from fleeing anywhere else."

Betha couldn't feel emotion across the distance, and

she realized she missed it. Part of her wanted to bask in Angie's faith that Carter would be okay. But just hearing it helped.

"You need to do what you need to do. Carter would understand. Just don't leave him there for too long. If you can drop him off with me once he is up, we could use the help," Angie said.

Betha listened intently as Angie explained the battle. With the portal no longer going to the Nexus, they couldn't get reinforcements from Terra. The small group had defended the portal so far, but it had been rough. They'd been attacked several times, and each time, the forces were stronger. Demons were actively searching for Betha. She was going to need to stay in the in-between if she was moving about.

"When he wakes up, I can bring him your way. I think I'm going to mostly be moving gargoyles to various portals, and I'm going to be staying in the in-between if I can. The demons can't follow me there," said Betha.

"Well, keep me in the loop. Good luck. I miss you."

"Thanks. I miss you too."

Betha pulled away from Angie and reached out for the map. The world that the king was on was connected to the fey wilds and the troll world. She was pretty sure it also connected to the dragnus world, though that portal was guarded by Balin. Plus the connections to the other Hells. It took her longer than she would have liked to figure out how to move around the map and zoom in and out. Betha wished her fireflies were here; they seemed to know what she meant when she tried things.

"Betha." Something touched her arm, and she

yanked away from the stone. Sir Samson swam in front of her and grabbed her arm. "You need to take a break and eat something." Her stomach took that moment to growl, and Betha noticed the light. It was getting close to sundown.

"Okay, yeah, time passes strangely while touching the stone." Her voice came out all dry, and Betha coughed. It must have been hours. Yet, she would have sworn it had been half an hour at most between the conversation with Angie and then moving the map around.

"That's okay. Lean on me. Let's go to the healer's room." Sir Samson steered her outside and to the building next door. It must have rained again—the stones in the road had puddles all over. A bright fire was going in the center of the healer's room, and something smelled very good.

Sir Samson sat her down on the bed next to Carter, then hurried off near the fire. He returned with a wooden cup of warm tea. "Drink that. I will get you some stew."

The tea smelled like cinnamon and maybe apples, but she couldn't be sure. It tasted good when she took a small sip. Her sips quickly turned into draining the cup.

"He spoke a bit in his rest," said Nalli, "which is a good sign. He hopefully just needs to rest, and I'm going to try to get some broth down his throat. Now, you also need to eat." She held out a bowl of stew she had taken from Sir Samson. Betha quickly grabbed it. "I don't know what you were doing, but just standing there for so long without moving isn't good for you."

Betha took a spoonful and wanted to swoon. It was

spicy and had some sort of meat in it. The stew was just what she needed. "I didn't realize it had been that long. Time kind of passed by. Time is a strange thing when dealing with different worlds and the in-between." She paused speaking to eat some spoonfuls of the food. It warmed her up nicely. Nalli didn't comment, and Betha glanced up to see that she had moved Carter to a seated position. She was working on getting spoonfuls of liquid between his lips.

"This is really good," said Betha.

"Thank you. I try to make things that people want to eat and will strengthen them all at once. Time passing without you knowing can be dangerous, Starwalker. Be careful."

Betha finished the bowl she had. "I will. I discovered there are only five portals from the world that the demon king is on. I have a few more things I want to study before finalizing plans. If I'm not back soon, come poke my arm."

Nalli nodded and kept at her task.

Betha headed back to the Sky Stone. She was disappointed that Carter wasn't awake yet. Part of her had hoped he would be up by the time she had gone back to the healer's room. She set her hands down and went back to studying the map.

Eventually, someone poked her and drew her back from the in-between. The doorway was completely dark, and someone had lit torches around the room. Nalli stood next to her, but she also had some watchers. Betha had thought the elder would have been with the volunteers. Six gargoyles stood in a group near the door.

"Betha, you need to take a break and meet some people."

"How long this time?"

"A few hours. The volunteers are here." Nalli motioned to the gargoyles.

"I only need four people—one is already protected by Balin," said Betha, a note of sadness in her voice.

One stepped forward at her words. She was Betha's height and seemed a little young. "I think I have been called, but I didn't want to touch the stone when you were working." The voice was soft, and Betha had to clench her fists. She was really young, maybe a teenager. If that. Betha stepped back from the stone, though. She was learning to honor their way, even if it was hard.

"What happened?" asked Betha. "To cause you to touch the stone?"

The young gargoyle flinched. "I had a burn from escaping the demons. It got infected on the way here. Nalli couldn't save me."

The healer beside her bowed her head. "I tried, my love."

"I know. I should have left with the others, but I wanted to help get the children here. It was worth it."

Betha's eyes grew wide at the exchange. Nalli and the young woman were related somehow. The young woman stepped up and touched the stone. Betha leaned forward at the sudden tug at her center. She couldn't resist her hand landing on the stone beside the young gargoyle's. The pathways flashed in her mind to the one portal she knew well. It was the one connecting the fey wilds and the Fifth Circle of hell. She snapped her hand back and shuddered.

"That's one of the ones you are trying to fill, isn't it?" asked the young woman.

Betha could only nod. Everything inside of her felt tight and twisted.

"Hey, it's okay." She touched Betha's hand. "I saved my sister from the demons. She is this big." She held her hand a few feet off of the stone floor. "I went into it knowing I was going to more than likely die. Instead, I got her out, along with myself, and we made it here."

Tears came to Betha's eyes.

"I have gotten a chance to find other family members and make sure she is safe. Now I get the chance to fight back and protect my people. Those who killed my parents and destroyed the village I have lived in my whole life. I can make a difference." Her eyes glimmered in the torchlight. "All of us have that chance, and you must let us take it," she added in a fierce whisper.

Betha nodded. Her eyes flicked to the rest of the gargoyles who had crept closer as the young one spoke. They were nodding with grins on their faces.

"Starwalker, we aren't fighters. Our people aren't warriors, but we can protect and guard. Let us," added another, a taller, young male gargoyle.

The tears rolled down Betha's face and she could only nod. She understood. She wasn't a fighter either. Not deep down. Betha fought because she had to, not because she wanted to. This was something they could do, and she needed to be okay with it. This was what *she* needed to do. These gargoyles needed to guard the portals, and she had to help them do it.

"I can get you there. One by one. And we will stop him from doing this again to another world."

"Shh, don't cry Betha," whispered a voice that brought her heart to her throat.

CHAPTER
TWENTY-TWO

Angie held the sword as she moved among the Guardd. They had lost four good people in the last fight, and several were wounded. A few of the Guards were moving the dead to a line off to one side. The flying creature was going from person to person, spreading dust, and it was helping. She didn't know how it was helping, but for those who weren't shifters, like the trolls and elves, it helped.

"Brutis, who do we have here?" asked Angie. "We need to have a better plan than just attacking things head-on."

The large black cat ran a paw along his ear and then shifted. "It's not like we have my team. We only have who was on this side. My team was coming on, but we weren't being careful about transfers. The portals don't go down." He was looking tired, and shifting back and forth wasn't helping.

Angie understood his frustration. This was a hot mess, and if they had worked from the knowledge that the portal could go down, a different protocol would have been in place.

"I get it, but who do we have *here*? Does anyone have magic? Any shifters who should change?" asked Angie. Her voice rang out over the group.

"I'm a witch and I have magic, but not the fighting kind." A woman stepped forward. "I was moving supplies over while going through basic training. I'm a support Guard."

That was not what they needed to hear, but Angie tried not to let it show on her face. "How many of you were here because of moving supplies?" Half of the Guards raised their hands. Most looked shell-shocked and had injuries. "What about the rest of you?"

"We were coming on duty," said a troll, standing up. "The group of us were part of the new team coming on. We are with Brutis." Brutis nodded at the troll. "Most of our shifters hadn't crossed yet."

"I was here," added another troll sitting on the ground. "And it was time for me to head back. I held off because we had members doing a patrol down the road. Given that they aren't back, I'm assuming they won't be." Angie moved to get a look at him. His arm was broken, but it was healing. "The shifters on the ground were with us." He motioned with his good arm to the deceased.

Three of the four people they had lost were shifters. The damage they had taken was just too intense, even for them. They had been protecting others, which made sense since most weren't supposed to be in battle.

"Support crew, let's chat about how you can help," said Angie.

"I'll keep a watch. My team, set a perimeter. Eyes open," said Brutis.

Angie motioned for the support team to move closer to the portal. It was time to be creative. They had to be to survive. They talked and planned until Angie hoped they had figured out a way to contribute.

She jumped when something nudged her hand. Brutis was back and she run a hand over his ears. He had a spot he loved to have scratched. He seemed calm, so trouble must not be super close. The cat pulled back as one of the shifters walked up.

"He says we have time, but not much. Demons are approaching from the north. The same direction as before. He snuck off and thinks it's around the same number as before. More of us are going to shift and hide in the bushes. Basically, make it look like we are worse off than we are."

Angie nodded. "That works with our plans. If needed, people will have to retreat through the portal back to Terra even though we don't know where it leads. We can hold the portal from the other side for much longer than this side but if it moves back to the Nexus we would be stranded. The fey are still out there—the ones that are helping us. And they really are helping us. Make sure no one touches anything but a demon."

He nodded. "All right, gonna shift now." He turned away and started to strip. The support crew jumped into action and grabbed his gear. One of them took up his sword. Angie could smell the demons now, and she stripped as well. The witch grabbed her clothing and put it in the pile with the others.

Her bones creaked as she shifted. While she had planned with the support crew, people had passed around rations and jerky. It was something, but eventually her tank was going to run dry. The shifters needed calories, especially after a fight. They didn't have a ton of food options ready to go, though. Those supplies must still be back at the Nexus. Angie shook out her fur once all four paws were on the ground and got ready. Food or not, they had to survive.

"Can I touch you?" asked the witch. Angie nodded. The witch's fingers ran through her fur. "You are amazing. This giant black wolf from lore." A smile came over her face. "Some members of the covens say you are bad luck. You never want to see the shadow wolf. But I don't think that is right. I think we're lucky as long as you are on our side. Happy hunting. May the fates guide your claws and each strike land true."

Angie blinked at the blessing. She felt the magic gather and land on her fur. Static moved along her paws, then settled. The witch wobbled a bit but steadied herself. "I wasn't sure if it would take, but I had to try."

She didn't know that any of the witches knew blessings. Angie had learned in history class that the witches could be dangerous warriors, depending on the goddesses they worshiped. Yet the witch hunts by the humans had reduced their numbers, and the witches had some weird rules about innocents. Still, she stood taller and wished she could thank the witch. Whether it would help her or not, it was well-intentioned and offered with grace.

Instead, she did what she did best and vanished into the shadows near the edges of the trees. The sun was closer to the horizon, and she prayed that they wouldn't still be here after dark. Right now, the shadows were long and she waited. Part of her wanted to go pick them off one by one, but she couldn't strike first. That was the rule, and they really, really didn't need more people upset with them.

One of the Guards moved into the clearing. Right where he couldn't be missed. Yet it dawned on Angie the demon's body was gone. The leader plus all of the others had vanished. She hadn't noticed until now. That seemed like something important. Angie moved deeper toward the demons that were coming. She only had to be close enough to hear the exchange.

Then the waiting began. It wasn't as long as she thought it would be. Hellhounds came first, but no imps this time. Just ten soldiers in black armor. She studied them, wondering who the leader was, but they all looked the same. That wasn't good.

They saw the Guard and halted.

"We wish you no harm, turn and go back where you have come from. You are not welcome on Terra." The Guard's voice was steady even though the likelihood of him getting out of this was low. The few shifters they had were in the bushes, and as soon as the demons attacked, everyone would fall back to the portal. Except for Angie.

The demons didn't say anything. Suddenly, they all

charged. The hellhounds took the lead. The shifters couldn't hide their scents as she could, and they ignored the Guard and went for the bushes. The Guard took off down the trail, and Angie heard the first yelp. That was her cue.

She stalked from the back. One by one, she would take them down. The farthest one, she yanked into the shadows of a tree. His death was quick in the shadow plane. Not one of the demons noticed. It made it easier to work her way through them as the shifters took out the hellhounds. Yes, they were outnumbered, but keeping them moving through the trees gave her time and space to work.

A sword flashed toward a wolf shifter, but it didn't land as Angie dragged the demon into the darkness. Angie smiled as she took him out. Yet, she noticed two dead wolves as the fight continued to move, both decapitated. At least five demons were down, and many hellhounds, but they were still losing. They couldn't replace their losses, and each death made the next fight harder.

They needed help.

BETHA WRAPPED her arms around Carter and did her best not to squeeze him too hard. It was so good to see his bright blue eyes. He rested in the bed Sir Samson had put him in. The fire flickered in the middle of the room, casting soft light over his face.

"I'm okay," he whispered. "Just need some rest. I will be as good as new."

"I'm so sorry."

"Not your fault. I should have been prepared for it to go sideways, though appearing several feet above the floor was not even a possibility that had occurred to me." It hadn't dawned on either of them that it wouldn't be like going through a portal. Though not all portals or tears existed in safe areas, the ones they had traveled had been relatively easy to access on both sides. Not to mention getting stabbed in the back by a surprised gargoyle. Poor Garson.

Betha filled him in on the plan to move the gargoyles through the in-between to the portals. "The goal is to not have to see any demons. The order has gone out to kill me, apparently."

"Don't die," he said. The lightness in his voice was betrayed by the deep feeling in his eyes.

"I won't. Angie is stuck on the fey wilds and has no way to get back to Terra. Or at least, no way to know where on Terra she would be if she went through the portal."

His eyes reflected the horror that she felt. "Kyra needs to get back and fix that. The portal area is not a place to take a stand."

Betha nodded. "Yeah, I really hope that she figures out what she needs to do. I'm worried about her."

"She is a fighter, and she knows where the safe zones are in the Fey Wilds."

"Angie isn't going to leave anyone behind," answered Betha.

Carter grimaced. "Well, you need to cut off the demons from the Fey Wilds, then."

Betha snapped her lips shut, but then shook her head. "I think I need to cut off the Fifth Circle of hell. If we don't, the king might flee from it to another one of the hells. I think the fey portal is going to be last."

He stayed silent, and Betha could feel the gears turning in his head.

"You're right," said Carter eventually.

"It sucks," replied Betha.

"She can hold on. You need to get moving. I will be fine here. Hopefully, in a few hours, I can join Angie. Right now, I would only hinder them."

Betha stood up and tried to give him a smile. Instead, tears came to the corners of her eyes.

"It will be okay, you got this." Carter pulled on her hand until she leaned over. His lips met hers and she couldn't help but soften. "Go trap the king."

"I will," she said.

Betha gave him one more look before heading out of the healing room. She almost paused when she caught sight of all of the gargoyles. They lined the walkway from the healer's room to the Sky Stone. The sky was filled with gargoyles flying about, and Sir Samson waited at the doorway to the round room.

"We are with you, Starwalker." The four volunteers were already in the room with the Sky Stone. Each had the compass rose painted on their chests in blue. The young female gargoyle had a flower crown on her head.

"Let's do this." Betha motioned for one of the gargoyles to come forward. "We are going to appear in darkness, flying. Don't let go of my hand, no matter what. I will get you to the portal."

He nodded. "Thank you, Starwalker. The honor is mine."

Betha grabbed his hand and then pictured the knife. It appeared in her fingers, and she heard a murmur among the gargoyles. She focused on the in-between, on the portal she could trace in her mind. Then they vanished. Betha relaxed as the darkness of the in-between came to her. The gargoyle jerked but did not let go of her hand.

"We are within the Tree," whispered the gargoyle.

"That's what Balin said. I don't see a tree. I see stars."

"I can't thank you enough for allowing me to see this. The stories whisper about it. How those who are heroes might get a glimpse when it is their time, but this..." Awe filled his voice, but Betha started moving. They were close to the portal she was aiming for. The bright doorway was up ahead. It connected to the troll world, and it was key for the trolls to eventually get their home back.

"This portal leads to the troll world on one side, and the Fifth Circle of hell on the other."

"I get to help the trolls?" asked the gargoyle. Betha nodded but didn't trust herself to say anything else. "One saved my life in the battle over the second portal. I fell from the sky, and one of my wings was torn. He caught me. Broke one of his arms, but he was happy to do it for his cousin."

Betha moved closer to the doorway. "Do you know what to do?"

He nodded. "I can hear it whispering to me. It is time." His fingers suddenly let go, and he walked along the path that glowed faintly in the light. He pulled a knife out of his pouch, and Betha flinched. Her eyes snapped shut but quickly opened as he spoke softly. The words were somehow lost, but the portal glowed a bright blue. Then he was gone.

The feeling of rightness washed over her. Betha took a deep breath and then focused on the Sky Stone. "Three more." Her words sounded loud in the darkness, but fireflies arrived in force. Her feet landed on solid stone, and someone steadied her shoulder. At least she didn't fall several feet to her knees this time.

"Starwalker, careful," whispered Sir Samson.

Betha glanced around. Three more gargoyles were left, yet the crowd of gargoyles still lined the walkway in multitudes. "Everyone is still here."

"We are with you through this. All of us," said the gargoyle who had first called her Starwalker.

Her fingers trailed over the Sky Stone, and Angie was back in her mind. Along with her distant bond to Eric.

"*Betha? Shit, Betha. Any updates on being trapped here? On Carter?*" asked Angie.

"*One portal down, three to go. He is resting—he can't stand yet.*"

"*Okay, we got this,*" Angie replied.

"*I gotta keep moving,*" said Betha, knowing the faster she finished, the sooner her friend could be safe.

"*Let me know when it is over,*" said Angie. Her friend felt tired, even though there was only a trace of any emotion coming through the bond.

"*I will. Stay safe,*" Betha said.

Eric blazed in the back of her mind, and she touched that connection.

"Betha, thank the fates! Are you okay? Something is wrong with Carter..." said Eric, trailing off. Concern rolled down the bond, and it brought a small smile to her face.

"Carter is okay. He hit his head a little hard and was stabbed. He is resting but healing well," replied Betha. *"Too much is happening to loop you in. Hopefully, soon we will be home."*

"Okay." He paused. *"Just make it back safe and sound, all of you. We both have a lot to talk about."*

"We will." Betha let go, and the map was gone, along with the connection. Carter was there, but she could feel he was resting. The connection to him was much stronger, and he felt more solid in her mind. Hopefully, that meant he would be good to go when she was. As much as she loved Sky World, they needed to get to Angie.

"All right, who's next?" asked Betha.

Another gargoyle stepped up. "I am, Starwalker."

Betha grabbed his hand. Then they were off. She could do this. They just had to keep moving.

CHAPTER
TWENTY-THREE

Something was different.

Ny didn't know what it was, but it tingled in the back of his mind. They had taken off and were heading toward the portal to the fey wilds. His wings beat in the air, and it was chilly up this high. He didn't get a chance to fly like this often. The king was on his back, but Ny did his best to ignore him. His order wrapped around his throat. To the fey wilds, they were going. Flying as quickly as they could to get the Traveler.

The Fifth Circle of hell wasn't his favorite, but it was better than the fourth. Whoever had been the native people on the fifth were completely gone. All of the goblins were dead. The demons had wiped them out. All that was left were rocks, mountains, and pathways. And a portal home. It was hidden in the mountains, but the demons couldn't get through it. The blue ones were safe. If he could get rid of the king, he could use that portal to return to his people. It was a dream, and maybe it was a possibility. For now, though, he pushed those thoughts out of his head. He had other things to focus on besides home.

The Fifth Circle was one of the hells that was used to travel through, but no one really stayed there since there wasn't any infrastructure. However, if the king was going to create a new family line, maybe he would give them this world to start on. It needed a people, or something. Something more than this empty stone. The more time he spent on this world, the more it screamed at him that it was wrong.

It dawned on him when that strange feeling washed over him again. He could always tell where the portals were on a world. It was something any dragnus could feel. They had changed. A few of the portals on this world now felt like the one that led to his world. Someone was protecting them. A shiver went down his spine. The fates were at work, and hope rose up within him.

Only two more to go. One that went to a world he had not been on, and then the one they were heading to. Maybe the king wouldn't be going into the fey wilds after all. Maybe this war could be averted.

THE NEXUS WAS a confusion of Guards, staff, and council members as a portal snapped into place. Kyra took a step on the stone floor, and everything went silent. James walked through after her, and she could feel the anger pouring off of him. The portal for the fey wilds appeared in its normal position.

"Someone has to go help our people!" growled James.

His voice rang in her head, echoing her own fear, but she ignored it. "James, just go. I'll handle this," she said.

His form shook, then a wolf tore out of his clothes. It set things in motion. The wolf ran through the portal at full speed. Kyra wished him luck as he vanished outside of her range. She moved to the center of the room and sat down on the floor, ignoring everything that was going on. Justin approached and sat down next to her.

"What happened?" asked Justin.

"Things outside of my control. We need to help our people, and then I can fix the Nexus."

"The council is in an uproar, but we have kept this from the humans. The treaty—"

"The treaty doesn't matter. Who came when we called for help? We sent messages, we asked for help with the demons, and who came?" Her voice shook as she replied. "Screw the treaty."

"I hope that isn't the official response," whispered Kellion.

Kyra hadn't even heard him approach. "I don't see any angels in the room willing to help the people in the fey wilds." In fact, he was the *only* angel in the room. Everyone else was Guard or council.

"That isn't our job," replied Kellion.

She raised her eyebrow. "Your job is to make sure the angels show up when we need help. They didn't. People died. Now you want access to our worlds and to continue your pilgrimages."

"Kyra." Justin's voice was tight, and she stopped talking. Another portal showed up—the one to the heavens.

Then the one to the elven woods. Kyra scoffed at the both of them and closed her eyes to focus.

"Lord Seth doesn't know that the portals vanished either. It was only for a few hours, and thankfully they are a bit busy at the moment," answered Kellion.

Justin let out a sigh, and Kyra resisted commenting. She shouldn't be picking fights right now, but everything inside her roiled. Andrea had lied. Kyra didn't need to stay here, attached to the Nexus. Things were going to change, and she just didn't care anymore. This was not going to be her life moving forward. That was it. She was done with this place. It had taken her heart, blood, and tears, not to mention two hundred years of her life. There wasn't anything else she was willing to give anymore.

James came to mind, and she didn't know what to do about him. The next steps were going to be hard, but at least she knew what she needed to do. More Guards moved through the portal to the fey wilds. It was time to get their people out of there and home, where it was at least safer. The fey could take care of themselves. If they wanted to trade with Terra, they could protect the portal.

"Where did you go?" asked Justin.

"None of your business," she snapped.

"Shifters saw someone grab you, and James didn't let go."

"I need to concentrate on getting the Nexus back to stability. Once that is taken care of, I need to speak to my Anchors."

Kellion softly gasped at that statement, and Kyra opened her eyes.

"What, not what you were expecting to hear?" she asked sarcastically.

Her anchors were a touchy subject, and most hadn't been seen in years. Not all of them had done well with the added years on their lives, and some weren't exactly what you'd call stable, or even sane. Either way, she didn't have enough anchors to do what needed to be done, and that meant she would need to find others as well.

Still, it was a path forward. One that was going to suck, but it was going to lead to her freedom.

And it would change everything.

GASPS AND SHOUTS came from back where the rest of the Guards were. Angie didn't let it break her focus. They just needed more time. Suddenly, a wolf appeared out of nowhere and dove right into the fight. The portal had to be back up.

She knew that wolf.

Angie darted out from the shadows and yanked another demon to the ground. She didn't get enough momentum to bring him into the shadow realm, but it didn't matter. Grandpappy jumped on him, tearing at his throat.

Cheers went up near the guards and Angie moved quickly away from the demons. She stepped out of the tree's shadow when she saw the reinforcements. With more people, the Guards made quick work of the demons that were left. Anyone who was down was quickly brought back through the portal for help. Grandpappy appeared by her side and nudged her. Angie moved toward the portal and shifted once she saw the spare clothing pile.

"I didn't expect to see you here," said Angie.

James shifted and grabbed a pair of too big pants. "I had to make sure that you were okay. We had gotten interrupted."

"I take it Kyra is back?" Angie asked.

"Yes. Her grandmother needed to have some words," James said.

"Betha said something like that," Angie said.

"Were they successful?" he asked.

Angie shrugged. "We'll see. She's been doing her thing in the Fifth Circle, but I know the one between there and here is still open." She really hoped he knew what she was talking about. There were way too many people nearby for her to speak freely. Not to mention, she didn't know who was in the trees.

The winged creature from before flew right in her face and bounced around. "Are you okay?" it asked in a squeaky voice.

Before she could respond, it darted down the path where Angie could now see something approaching. It was a giant grizzly bear with vines growing out from under its fur. Piercing green eyes stared out from the mass of fur and plants. Vines twisted and turned on the ground, trailing from the creature. Massive claws grew out of the paws. The creature flexed its claws and shifted. A haze flowed over him and, the next moment, it was a tall, pale man. His head was covered with thick green hair that reached his waist. Sharply pointed ears poked out of his great green mane. When he smiled, he showed slightly pointed teeth. It was not a gentle smile, but it didn't seem to convey malice, either. At least, not toward their group. He had on brown trousers and a cream-colored linen shirt. A scabbard hung around his hips with a blade. His feet were bare.

More things were in the trees, but Angie didn't know what they were, only that they were watching. Flashes of green and brown eyes appeared here and there. For a second, she swore she saw the green man who had escaped with Leina and Ayda. She stepped in front of the Guards.

"Shadow Fen," said the fey, nodding slightly in acknowledgment. Angie felt Grandpappy flinch behind her. Angie realized this was the creature who had followed them through the wilds. He had protected them.

"I have been told not to leave the path," she replied, making it clear she understood the rules.

"One such as you walks where they need to," replied the fey. "I am surprised to see one of your kind here. This world will never need your touch as long as we lords live. Will you join us? The demons have broken the agreement. We are cleansing our land of the stain of their evil."

Angie turned toward Grandpappy, her eyebrows drawn.

"Keep in touch with Betha. It will help what she is doing," he said. She nodded.

"I will join you for this hunt," Angie said to the green-haired being.

The fey nodded and strode off into the trees. As he approached the edge of the path, the trees moved, and a trail was created for him.

"What was that?" asked Angie.

"You need to go. I swear once you are back—and you better come back—we can talk. Be safe, bunny," said Grandpappy.

Angie yanked the shirt over her head and shifted back to wolf form. The back-and-forth was wearing her out, but she didn't have a choice. She nudged Grandpappy's hand and then ran down the path to catch up. He hadn't called her bunny in a long bit. For some reason, he thought this was important for her to do.

Whatever was running in the trees with them picked up speed as she joined what must be a fey lord. The trees kept moving out of his way. An imp was thrown into the middle of the path, and she swore a bush had pushed it there. The lord yanked a sword out and sliced it in two before it could make a sound. Vines yanked the body beneath the dirt, leaving no trace.

Angie's blood was pumping, and it felt like a full moon hunt in the forest. The pack would work together to bring down prey and then feast, and while she had no desire to eat this prey, it was definitely a hunt.

Energy ran up her paws and eased the fatigue that had been creeping up on her. The sound of imps being torn apart under the cover of the trees shocked her. Other demonic creatures were dumped into the path, and the fey took care of each. Then something bigger dropped down in the middle of the path, and the fey paused his march forward. It was a demon, but not one of the soldiers. He had on black armor and crawled on all fours. It stared at the fey before bowing its head.

"What are you doing in my land?" The question hit like a shock wave, and Angie had to resist stepping back. If that power had been directed at her, she would have answered without hesitation. The demon didn't have a prayer of resisting.

"Hunting," the creature said fearfully.

"That is not part of the agreement. What prey do you seek?" asked the fey.

"Traveler, bring it to the king." His head sunk toward the ground. "Get family line."

Angie froze, and her eyes narrowed on the demon. They were hunting Betha. She didn't even realize she was growling until the demon glanced her way. Now would be a great time for Betha to pop into her connection so she could warn her again.

The fey turned to her, his eyes glowing. "This one is yours," the tall, elegant creature said, indicating the demon cowering before him.

Angie moved before the sentence was complete. The demon didn't stand a chance. She dug her teeth into its throat. The brackish blood filled her mouth and splattered across the clearing before she let the demon fall. The fey stared at her for a moment and nodded before continuing on his march. More vines creeped out of the underbrush, and Angie noticed they were connected to a bright blue flower. One of the many singing flowers they had seen on their way through the Fey Wilds. Angie stepped back from the demon's body as the flower slowly pulled the body toward its roots. Dirt moved to cover the rest.

Nothing made sense anymore. The flowers were eating demons. The power that had come off of the fey was intense. Not to mention he had called this *his* land. Dread almost trickled down her spine, but she pushed it away. She didn't have the time or the energy to deal with it. Right now, she needed to focus on the fey lord and the portal they must be heading to.

The sounds coming from the trees increased. There were screams of things getting torn apart, crunches of broken bones, and the sounds of great trees shifting and moving at the will of the fey lord. Carter had been right —you didn't want to piss off the fey.

TWENTY-FOUR

Betha was running on empty. She appeared next to the Sky Stone, and cheers rose up. Someone pushed a mug of something into her hand. She didn't even blink before downing it. Carter was right there, along with Sir Samson, Nalli, and Talli.

"Can you take a break?" asked Carter. He stood next to the stone. He looked almost normal, but something was different.

"I don't know if we have time," she said, gasping a little.

Her fingers touched the stone, and power rushed up through her.

"Angie, updates?"

Excitement, focus, and determination rolled down the bond.

"Uh, a fey lord is pissed. Cleaning the Fey Wilds of demons. The king is invading."

Betha's hand trembled. They needed the king on the

other side of the portal. Leaving him in the Fey Wilds wasn't going to work. *"Where is he?"*

Angie pushed a picture down the bond, and the image of the king flying through the air on the back of the dragnus showed up.

"What is he even trying to do?" asked Betha.

"No idea, but he wants you dead. He is throwing away demons at this point."

"I can't trap him there—he has to be on the other side of that portal," Betha said.

"Shit," Angie said. Clearly, that wasn't what she had wanted to hear. Angie went silent and Betha froze, waiting. She couldn't seal the last portal until the king was no longer in the Fey Wilds.

"I'll let you know if he crosses," her friend said eventually. It was going to have to do.

Betha didn't want to let go of the Sky Stone, but she had to. She glanced at the teenager. "We need to go. The king is in the Fey Wilds, but he's being fought by a fey lord. As soon as he crosses back, we need to seal it up."

The gargoyle nodded, and a little one darted out of the crowd. "You are going?" asked the gargoyle child.

"It is time, little bat," said the teenager in her ceremonial paint.

"I miss you." The small one looked down, her toe digging in the dirt.

"I'll miss you too. I love you so much," replied the teenager. She reached out and touched the child's chin, bringing her eyes up to look deep into them. "You know the words, little bat. What are they?"

"To the sky?" said the young one in a small voice, clearly trying not to cry.

"To the sky," echoed her older sister as she hugged the little one close. Then she let her go, and the little gargoyle ran back into the crowd to find her family.

Betha felt Carter squeeze her hand. She turned toward him, and he wrapped her in a hug. "You got this. Don't forget me here," he said, a grin in his voice.

"I couldn't forget you anywhere. Ever," said Betha.

He kissed her forehead and pulled back. Sir Samson gave her a nod.

"Let's do this," Betha said, reaching for the teenager.

Betha had gotten better at traveling with the knife. It was different from traveling other ways, and it pulled at different places inside of her. The energy drain was the worst, and she wasn't sure if she could keep it up without the Sky Stone. She had almost tried to take all the gargoyles at once, but something warned her not to try. Not yet.

Only a moment later, the portal glowed in front of them. Betha had brought them nearly right to it, and the gargoyle tried pulling away. "Not yet. We need to wait until it is time," Betha said. She tightened her grip on the young gargoyle's hand.

"How will we know?" she asked.

Betha approached the edges of the portal, and the knife vanished. With her free hand, she touched the edges of the white light.

"*Let me know when he is through,*" she sent to Angie. The waiting was always the worst. But this was it. Her plan was going to work. She could feel it.

THE TREES SUDDENLY STOPPED. They were like a row of soldiers lining the ridge. She skidded to a stop as the fey lord paused before stepping out to the bare ground. Smoke and the screams of unknown creatures filled the air. The flap of wings overhead made her want to hide under the canopy behind them.

The fey lord stood tall. A breeze picked up, pushing the smoke away. If a wolf could gasp, she would have. A stone archway contained a massive portal, one of the biggest she had seen. It was still some distance away, but easily visible from where she stood. Demons poured out of the sparkling light, all in black armor and helmets. The eyes under the helmet brims glowed a variety of colors. Imps flew in the air above them, and some other creatures wandered around by their feet. There were so many, it was hard to pick out what was what.

There were too many. This was an army.

Angie huffed and then shifted. She did not want to lose her wolf advantages, but they needed to make a game plan, and talking while in wolf form was not possible, even with this fey. There were just so many bodies. Overhead, the sound of wings grew louder, and she spotted the dragnus.

"He doesn't look like he is trying to escape," muttered Angie.

"The dragnus is enslaved. The noble creature is trying not to hit any of my trees," said the fey lord.

Once he pointed it out, she could see that the dragnus wasn't using his fire on the trees but was just getting really close. The trees literally leaned out of the way. It was creepy.

"I haven't seen one in so long. Our trade with them was cut off when the demons took over the route through the goblin lands."

"How are we going to do this?" asked Angie.

A smile crept over the fey lord's face. Tiny vines in his green hair shook. He was laughing at her. "You are here to witness, not to fight, Shadow Fen. I will not let the magic fall from this world. We are connected to the Tree, and strong."

A yell came from above, and Angie stared at the king, who was on the dragnus' back. His dark armor blended in with the dragnus' scales, but red light flickered from his crown.

"Stand witness," said the fey lord. The very air seemed to freeze in place, but the dragnus kept flying. Angie's eyes grew wide as energy gathered around the fey Lord.

AKELDAMA SNUCK across the lands of hell. Normally she would march down the main roads, but she wasn't sure if her father had spies in the motherland. Only the strongest of demons lived here. This was their home. She had grown up in the palace before she had grown old enough to rule over the Twilight World, which was the Second Circle of hell. Ever since Akeldama was little, she had loved the purple skies, the darkness, and the quiet of the Twilight World.

Still, part of her had always ached for this world—the First Circle—the home world of the demons. The sky gray lightened in the morning, and the rocks were dark, some sparkled with reds. The stories all said that the very rock would vary according to the nature of the king or queen who commanded, shifting with each change of reign.

Small domains were speckled about. Lieutenants and leaders from the noble houses all had holdings here. Each of the holdings dug deep into the rock. The surface was only for the high bloods. Underneath was where the lower classes were. As magnificent as some of those holdings were, they were all dwarfed by the palace.

The back wall to the palace gardens was ahead. A quick trip through it and then she would be back to where she had been born. The tugging in her chest guiding her had increased once she had crossed over into this world from her own, and she knew it would be over soon, one way or another.

Storm clouds towered over the building, causing her to pause. This was new. White lightning crackled overhead. As soon as she paused, the tugging in her chest caused her to stumble forward. Akeldama climbed to her feet and headed to the gate in the wall. She didn't have time to wait.

The gardens were dark as the plants twisted and turned in the winds that had picked up. The doors to the throne room were wide open. The room was dark, but she could see figures lining the way up to the chair. Glowing eyes in the darkness—reds, blues, greens, and even some whites. A flash of lightning showed that the heads of all of the most important noble houses were here. Then she realized it wasn't just the heads—the oldest of them were here as well. The sleeping ones and those who could not leave this world.

No one moved as she entered the room. Her chest buzzed, and she felt the connection to the throne. Two figures flanked it, both sworn to her father. They growled in the darkness, attention going to an unknown sound. Akeldama, head held high, stepped in the aisle between the first two court members. They didn't move.

The pull increased, and she kept going. Her eyes stayed on the throne, the pull from her chest turned visible, glowing in the darkness. When she hit the halfway point, dark purple light flickered between her and the throne. At that moment, the princess of hell felt eyes on her from all directions. Things that hid in the darkness and depths of this hell, and the things that stood tall in this room. The old ones focused on her back, but they didn't move.

The lieutenants locked eyes with her. One moved to try to intercept her path. She drew her sword. Akeldama hadn't even realized she had moved before he turned into dust. Black light danced along her blade, and she kept it out. The second bowed his head as she took the first step, then the second.

Akeldama sent out her call to Typhon. When she reached the fifth step, he was there by her side, one step behind her.

Dust rained down as the crown on her head crumbled. A breeze blew the ash away as she turned. The old ones faced her as she sat down on the throne. All those eyes glowing in the darkness—some slitted, others solid orbs of color—continued staring at her.

It was time. The queen of hell smiled as a new crown grew out of her skull, proof that her power was now greater than her father's. The pain, inconsequential, throbbed at the top of her head. Purple light consumed the room, and the bonds of order snapped into place from one demon to the next. *Her* army was in need of new orders.

Long live the queen.

THIS WAS NOT GOOD. Ny flew through the air and did his best to not let his fire touch the trees. His people had spoken of the Fey Wilds and trading with the lords, of earning hunting privileges and trading carcasses with them. They were one of few creatures that seemed to understand the flying giants, and one of the few races that could match their power. And here he was, using his flame near their forest. He only hoped the fey he'd heard so much about understood that he had no choice.

If he died here, he was taking the king with him.

Each tree jumped out of the way, and he prayed to the fates that they could feel his reluctance. The king on his back ordered more and more demons through the portal. There couldn't be many left in the Fifth Circle, or even the Fourth, unless they were rebelling against the king. It was strange, but it seemed demons were missing. Not all of the symbols of the different houses had shown up. And those who had were foot soldiers, not the more senior ranks.

None of the riders, vanishers, or magic users had come. The prince had decimated the creature population from the Third Circle that he had ruled. So while there were some imps, hounds, and cats, there weren't nearly as many as were needed for this sort of battle.

"There is the forest lord!" yelled the king.

Magic gathered around the king, and Ny's scales itched. The oily feel of the magic made him want to dive into a burning lake and wash it away. Instead, he kept flying back and forth. The noise increased as the demons stepped forward as one.

The magic flashed red, and Ny almost crashed to the ground as the king's loud voice echoed from his back. His ears hurt and had to be bleeding, it had been so loud.

"I want the Traveler!" yelled the king's magically enhanced voice.

His demand rolled across the battlefield, and Ny flew lower. It had almost driven him to the ground, but he shakily recovered. Without orders, he flew over the demon troops and hovered with his back to the portal. He knew right where it was in case he had a chance to flee.

No response came from the fey lord, but Ny didn't expect anything. The demons were so pitifully outnumbered, and the king didn't even realize it. How could someone be so dumb?

Power rippled across the field, but nothing physical happened. Ny bowed his head slightly as the troops marched farther on. The imps and crawlers went first, heading directly to the forest where the lord stood. A naked woman stood near the lord, which was strange, but she was several steps behind. Maybe a pet of some kind? Suddenly, the ground opened up wide and vines shot out, taking all of the creatures within reach. It then snapped shut as if it was a mouth that had fed. The suddenness of it and the single, reverberating *crack* it made were a more elegant demonstration of power than Ny had seen in some time.

Hesitancy filled the air. Nothing immediately came from the king, and Ny wanted to smile a toothy smile. The tales from his ancestors had made it clear the fey, and especially the fey lords, were not to be trifled with. More red light flickered overhead and then down to the troops. They moved forward again, but it was with smaller steps. The cohesiveness had been broken, and they were clearly hesitating despite the command of the king.

"Charge!" yelled the king.

The order rolled across the battlefield, and many did charge, but not all. Amazingly, some held their ground or even began to back up until the weight of those behind pushed them forward. The king was not being obeyed, at least not by all. The king's heels dug into his side, and Ny jerked upright in the air. More red light flickered, and the ones who were resisting fell into line on the ground.

Quietly, the king directed Ny to back up closer to the portal. The bonds that wrapped around him weren't as tight as usual. Ny obeyed since it made sense to get closer to escape, but it was clear the king had wanted him to move more quickly. There was a twinge of the usual pain, but it wasn't as strong or sharp as it had always been. A ripple crossed the soldiers as they approached the line where the mouth had formed in the ground, and some began to hesitate again.

Then it happened. They pushed back on the order en masse.

Ny didn't wait—he bucked into the air, trying to dislodge the king. Then he rolled midair to try to get the hated demon off of his back. This was his chance, and he was not going to lose it. Pain stabbed into the brand in his mouth, and blood flowed between his teeth. His bones felt like they were burning. He wanted so much to be free, but the binding was too tight. He couldn't control himself as he stopped bucking. The king took control, and Ny darted through the portal with the king still on his back.

The transition to the Fifth Circle was rough, and he barely stayed in the air. In the end, he didn't quite manage it. His face hit the empty road in front of him as pain flowed into his body from the brand. His eyelids rapidly closed and opened, not under his control. Yet he did notice one thing. A very big thing. In the distance, the giant portal they had just come through flickered from the bright white of an open portal to the blue of a guarded one.

CHAPTER
TWENTY-FIVE

Waiting was the worst. But there wasn't much else that Betha could do. Wait and watch. Which was also what Angie was doing. Seeing her Anchor standing naked in the distance next to what had to be a powerful fey was strange.

Yet here she was waiting for the king to go back through the portal. This was the strangest battle. It seemed no one wanted to be here but the king.

Then it happened. The great dragnus tried to get rid of the king. As he flew directly into the portal, Betha could see the blood dripping down between his teeth.

She pulled back as they passed through and squeezed the gargoyle's hand. "All right, it's time."

"Finally," the youngster said.

"He's through now—go."

The gargoyle touched the portal, and Betha prayed to the fates that this would work. So much was depending on this. It flickered to blue, and she couldn't catch what the girl was saying. Instead, a bright smile came over her face, and she vanished into bright white light.

Emotions boiled up in Betha, but she locked them down. Now was not the time for that. Instead, she touched the portal and peered back out to the Fey Wilds. Purple light was flickering over the demonic soldiers, and most were fighting each other or scrambling back toward her and the portal. They passed through easily, which meant that they weren't trying to start trouble.

The purple light caught her attention. It was new. Before, it had been red. Something had to be happening in the Fifth Circle. Fireflies rose all around her as she peeked at the other side into that lifeless world.

In the distance, she could see a black heap crashed next to some large stones. Demons were streaming into the world but weren't heading anywhere near the great black mound. Instead, they all seemed to be marching as fast as they could toward a different portal. The one leading to a different circle of hell. That portal was also blue, but nearby. It shocked her how fast they were moving. That strange purple light was still flickering over their armor.

"Get up!" yelled a harsh voice.

Betha's attention moved back to the black heap. The dragnus slowly climbed to its feet and what had to be the king climbed on its back. He took to the air, but slowly, barely staying off of the ground and above the rocks. He headed not toward the nearby portal as the rest of the demons were, but closer to the one to the troll home world.

Something was up.

The dragnus could barely move in the air. Everything pulled at Betha. She needed to get back to the Sky Stone, and Angie was still in the Fey Wilds, but she had promised to try to free Nyducrin. Then, if she could, help him get back to his home world.

"What should I do?" she asked the in-between all around her.

The fireflies didn't give her an answer, but she felt like she had to try. Betha nodded to herself, and the knife appeared in her hand. At least she had her sword and armor on, though how much good they would do if the dragnus attacked her was questionable. After a deep breath, she vanished from the in-between.

The air was dry as she landed, and the wind was intense, but at least she was on her feet. Fatigue washed over her, and she wondered if this was a mistake. The thought that she could leave if she needed to was all that kept her creeping forward. When she had concentrated on the knife, she had asked to go to where Nyducrin was.

Giant rocks surrounded her and blocked her view, but she could hear something. Someone was screaming in rage. Betha quietly moved toward the sound. It was very close. She peeked around a rock and saw the dragnus perched on a large boulder. The King was literally throwing rocks at the creature, screaming. Something was different, and it only took a moment for Betha to notice that the King's crown was gone. It had been hard not to notice it during the battle, with its red light. Now, nothing sat on his head. He looked strange without it.

His red eyes frantically darted around as he ran out of

rocks. His chest rose and fell quickly as he stumbled about. Then his screaming cut off as he gasped for breath. He turned toward the side, and Betha noticed a cave opening. The former king made his way toward it. The dragnus didn't move, and from what she could see, the great beast's eyes were closed.

Blood still dripped from between his teeth, but not as much as before. The rocks had bounced off his thick hide, but that still had to have hurt. Betha didn't know how to approach him. All she needed was for him to call the king out.

Nyducrin had failed. It was all for naught. The demon could still order him about even after the crown had crumbled. Red light did not spark from it, and the king had turned to throwing rocks at him. Yet, as he barked orders, the dragnus still had to obey.

It hurt.

His soul hurt.

He had gotten so close. Seeing the soldiers resist had given him hope, and he had given it his all. In trying to get away from the king, he had caused himself great pain. But it hadn't been enough. The roof of his mouth burned, and he wished he could get some water to rinse the blood off of his tongue. The king had wandered off, but he dare not leave the rock he was told to sit on. He couldn't take much more.

Maybe it was time to rot and just wither away.

"*Nyducrin,*" whispered a very small voice. The fates

were finally calling his name so he could rest. *He could let his mind go. They were here.*

"*I'm here to help you get home to Ythe,*" said the small voice.

That was not the fates. The voice had come from off to his side. He opened his eye closest to the voice and realized a creature was perched behind a rock. Power ebbed and flowed around the small creature, and its eyes stared into his.

"*We need to get you home,*" stated the little thing.

There was no way for him to get home. Not with this brand in his mouth. He was forbidden to remove it.

It moved closer to him, and he could feel the energy coming off of it. Whatever it was, it had power. It felt like the portals. He cracked open his mouth and took a deeper breath. It even tasted like the portals—warmth, fire, and that moment before you bit into a perfectly cooked piece of meat.

"*Can you understand me?*" Somehow he could, and that spooked him. His people spoke in growls, roars, and shouts, but also inside each other's heads. This was where her voice was, soothing inside his mind. Like one of his people was here with him.

"*How can I get you out of here? You have to be marked somewhere. I just need to find it.*"

She knew that he was branded. Shame rolled over him, but he felt a touch near his eye. "*Don't you dare give up. I'm going to get you out of here. Watch out for the demon.*"

He didn't like orders, but what she said made sense.

This little creature was here for him. Someone knew he was here and wanted to help.

"It is in my mouth," he whispered back just like he was talking to a dragnus. It was how he had whispered to the elven healer.

"That's why you are bleeding. Can you show me? It might hurt, but I need to burn it off."

"Carve it. I can't be burned," he replied.

He watched as she flinched. Interesting. She didn't want to hurt him, and it bothered her that she would have to. How did one still so good find her way to this horrible place? It was dangerous for those with kind souls to travel the lands. He opened his mouth and tried not to breathe out of it. Instead, he focused on breathing through his nose.

Ny didn't miss the very small gasp as he did. She was like a mouse afraid to approach a wounded cat. Not that he liked having his mouth filled with blood, either.

"It is on the roof," he said to the thing.

"I see it. I have to step inside. Please try not to eat me—this might hurt," it said.

There was no might about it. It was going to hurt, but he could put up with the pain. He opened his mouth wider as she stepped closer. Ny froze as much as possible.

"Can you close your mouth a little? I'm short and need to be able to reach. I don't want to climb all the way in. No offense."

Ny almost laughed. This still didn't seem real, but he did as she asked. He could feel something touching the roof of his mouth and his tongue. It was strange. One didn't play with one's food, and usually nothing alive was in his mouth very long.

"Here I go," it said.

Something small pierced his mouth, and he dug his claws into the stone. It wasn't as bad as what the king had done, but he was scared he would hurt the creature and it would stop. Instead, it moved quickly. Almost as soon as it started, though, he heard the sound of footsteps approaching from the cave.

"The demon is coming," whispered Ny. *"You need to run."*

"Almost got it," the little one said.

Then everything changed inside his brain. It hurt, but now the little thing was climbing out of his mouth.

"You need to fly. Go home!" it said to him.

Even now, the little mouse ordered him around. This time to leave it behind. He would not do that.

"What do we have here?" said a harsh voice into the silence.

Ny turned toward the sound, and everything in him stood at attention. The king was back. He had a sword out and pointed at the little creature. The king was so large compared to his small savior.

The creature didn't speak, just took a step away from Ny.

"Ny, you need to go," it said again.

Ny roared. It echoed around the rocks and sounded so beautiful to him. It was the sound of being free, of having a choice. And he had a choice. The king was not going to touch the little mouse.

Harsh laughter came out of the king, and power

gathered around him. "Stay!" He commanded Ny. The king took another step forward, red light flickering over his sword. "I'll now get another knife and get out of this world."

The creature took another step back and held out a small knife. Ny could see the blood on it. She had used that instead of the much nicer sword at her side to get the brand off of him.

"No, you won't." She spoke the same language as the demon.

Ny couldn't handle it anymore and flicked his tail out. It slammed into the king, knocking him into one of the boulders near the cave entrance. Ny climbed off of his boulder and slowly crawled toward the king, who was trying to get to his feet. That wouldn't do.

His claws made quick work of tearing the king out of his armor. He didn't want to play with him, but there was only so much one could take before one had to fight back. He dug into the king's head and squeezed. Seeing the mess, he quickly blew fire over the remains, turning him into ash.

"*Feel better?*" asked the mouse.

Ny realized the small creature was still there, watching from his boulder. She had taken a seat at some point. That pure soul couldn't be here, not with all of the demons crossing this world. It wasn't safe. He jumped into the air. She stood and waved at him as he circled.

Then he dove.

TWENTY-SIX

Betha giggle. She'd only resisted since she didn't know how Nyducrin would respond. He had scooped her up in his claws and headed directly to the portal that led to his world.

This was not how she thought this would turn out. It was clear he didn't know what she was or that she could leave at any point. Still, she resisted leaving. He was being really careful about his claws, and she could feel that he was trying to get her to safety. He didn't want her to get hurt, especially after freeing him from the brand of the king. And she was tired. That last trip with the knife had been a bit much. When the king had shown up, she didn't know if she could make it anywhere but to the in-between.

Though he wasn't a king anymore, or even alive. Nyducrin had taken care of that. That demon king who had caused so much trouble was now ash. From their height in the sky, she could see demons streaming toward one porta that led to one of the demon worldsl much farther in the distance. The princess must have kept her word. She was pulling back the demons.

Though, she was probably queen now.

Betha glanced toward the portal that led from the troll world, but nothing was leaving it. She knew there had been plenty of demons there. What she didn't understand was why they weren't leaving. The thought left her mind as the portal to Ythe loomed closer.

"*Betha?*" It was the voice of a friend, one she hadn't wanted to let go, but who had fulfilled his own destiny.

"*Balin. He is free and going home,*" Betha told her gargoyle friend, Guardian of the portal to Ythe. Betha could only smile as they passed through the bright blue surface of the portal. His joy was contagious. She gasped as the portal faded behind them. The sky was so blue that the white clouds seemed to glow. And the mountains! Giant hunks of rock floating in the air. Some small, like the size of a car, others bigger than buildings with flat surfaces. They floated in the air, vines trailing down, sometimes connecting them. In the far distance, she could see even more mountains, but she wasn't sure if they touched the ground. The portal behind her was connected to a floating rock face.

Ny's whole body shook as he roared into the air. This was amazing, but she couldn't stay. Given the time it had taken for him to dispatch the demon and then get here, she was pretty sure she had rested enough that she could get back to the Sky Stone. Carter was waiting for her.

"*Nyducrin, I need to go,*" she said, then paused, wondering how to phrase this. "*My family is waiting for me. I...*" Her words faded as dark shapes rose in the clouds, and she could make out giant wingspans.

"*You are safe, little mouse.*"

"*I know that, great Nyducrin. My goal was to make sure you made it home. I will see you again, but for now, goodbye.*"

Betha smiled as another dragnus headed their way, voice blasting across the air.

"*My son! You are home!*"

The knife glowed in her fingers, then she was gone.

THE POOR DRAGNUS had tried to remove the king from his back. The fey lord had pushed the winds out to give him a hand. Unfortunately, it was for naught, as the dragnus and the demon had vanished through the portal. The demons on the ground fought amongst themselves. It was such a waste of life, even demon life. Thrown away by a ruler who didn't understand what it meant to rule.

At least the lord's lands would flourish. Vines crept along the edges of the fighting demons, yanking them into the trees. His people waited under the cover of the treetops for their pound of flesh. The rose fey had gathered en masse, and the fey lord grabbed several demons to send their way. The trees themselves were rumbling. The ground shook, and the demons cowered. This was not a safe place for their kind.

The lord did not move from his spot next to the Shadow Fen. Instead, he stared at the portal. He had felt the power of the prior king fade. Another had taken the demonic throne. Though, the portal glowed a faint blue.

The demons wouldn't be able to use this pathway into his lands. If they wished to travel to his lands, they would need to find a path through the lands of one of his siblings. He would have to warn them that they might try.

Demons scrambled toward the portal as more and more of them were dragged into the underbrush. Screams rose from the shadows where the fey took care of the demons. The Shadow Fen beside him had to return home.

"My lands will be cleared within the night. The evil stain is gone." The rage inside him had settled down, and his internal balance was restored. It would be centuries before he could sleep again. For now, he needed to travel his lands, reassuring his people and helping them heal. Not to mention send someone to talk to those at the Nexus. They had upheld their bargain at the cost of many lives, and it had been close. They had given much, yet the neutral ground around that portal might need to shrink. The treaty ways were open, but he would need to keep a better eye on who was traveling through his lands.

"Let us walk." He motioned to the way he had come with the Shadow Fen. They had stood witness and now knew his lands were secured. He was no longer worried about the fates interfering in his domain. However, the crossroads world beyond the now-guarded portal would be a problem. Especially if the dragnus prince managed to get free of its chains. If the crossroads world fell to the Shadow Fen, then he wouldn't get visits from his majestic friends. The dragnus would need to pass through it to visit.

The Shadow Fen with him shifted into her wolf form for the walk back. That was fine, even if she didn't want to talk, she could listen, and maybe he could save that world as well.

"The crossroads world is dangling by a thread. You will visit it soon. It should be saved. That pathway to the trolls and dragnus could be invaluable to those on Nexus."

It was good to be back on all four paws. That way, she wasn't as tempted to ask any of the questions that were bubbling up inside of her. The fey lord had let the demons fight among themselves for only a few minutes before the ground shook. At that point, the ones not already racing toward the portal quickly followed their more attentive fellows.

The portal to the Fifth Circle was glowing a light blue, and that felt good. She knew there was a gargoyle behind it and that they were serving their purpose. It was important. Now her only job was to get back to Terra. Grandpappy had answers, and she had way too many questions.

Yet, despite how important that was, it wasn't what she kept coming back to as she padded along the trail. What she kept coming back to was exhaustion. They had been traveling for what seemed like forever, and she needed to rest. Sleep, true, but more than that, just not be in a crisis for a day or two. Or a year or two, maybe. Angie's stomach growled, and almost every part of her ached. The fey lord kept pace with her this time, and the forest was quiet.

The trees were also not moving back into place. A trail was left to the portal, nice and wide like the one to the desert world that eventually went to Sky World. It was good she couldn't ask why. The fey lord had spoken of that world, and she had listened to him. He knew something, but she didn't trust herself to ask questions. It was why she had shifted. Sometimes the price of knowledge was too high.

But she couldn't deny that she could feel the portal, the one to the Fifth Circle of hell. It was like a dot in the back of her mind that didn't move. It itched. Her nose wanted to sniff it.

It was strange. She had never *felt* a portal before. Something was different about that world, and the wolf part of her needed to know. Her tiredness won over her new sensations, but after enough time, she knew she would be back.

TWENTY-SEVEN

Betha didn't want to move from the couch. She had sat down as soon as she'd let Eric know they were back on Terra. He was on his way. She sank lower into the red couch and closed her eyes. A couch had never been so comfortable before. After weeks of sleeping on the ground or on beds made of straw, this was pure luxury.

Kyra had let them into her private rooms off of the Nexus since none of them wanted to speak to anyone outside their little circle. It was a sparse living room with a kitchen on one side. The sitting area had a massive u-shaped couch around a low coffee table. The kitchen had a big island with plenty of seating. Several guest rooms were just down the hall, each outfitted with a bed and a dresser. It seemed like such a large space for only one person.

People had crowded around her and Carter as soon as they had appeared in the Nexus. As soon as Kyra saw them, she had cleared everyone out and directed the two of them here. Angie had taken a shower and was now sitting on the couch next to Betha. Her friend's clothes were somewhere, but for now, she had on gray sweats and a tank top. Carter was taking a turn getting clean. Kyra had mentioned food was on the way before she left them here to go send the mob of interested parties on their way. Their giant pile of weapons sat on the island in the kitchen, and to Betha's shock, Angie had gotten a sword from somewhere.

"We did it," said Betha.

Angie nodded, brushing her long hair. "Not in a way I thought we would, but we did. Ding dong the king is dead, the wicked king," she said as a grin crept over her face.

Betha chuckled. Trapping him had been her goal, not killing him, but she couldn't fault Ny for tearing into him. Not at all. That brand on the roof of his mouth had been horrible. No one deserved that. The shower cut off, and Betha pulled herself to her feet. She was the next one up. Before she made a step, there was a knock at the door causing her to turn in that direction.

Grandpappy opened the door with boxes of pizzas in his arms. "You guys aren't going to believe who I recruited to help." Right after him, Joey appeared with even more boxes.

"As soon as he said garlic knots—I knew you guys had to be back." His voice was soft as he stared at Angie. The brush in her fingers slipped to the floor with a thud. "Is everyone back?" He glanced between the two of them, and then Carter came out of the bathroom. "Perfect.

Everyone made it safe and sound. I can stop worrying now."

He set the boxes of food on top of what Grandpappy had set on a table and took a seat on the couch next to Angie. Betha didn't move as he wrapped his arms around her friend, and she leaned into his shoulder. The kiss he gave her forehead was sweet.

"Well," interrupted Grandpappy, "I have food, and we have more to discuss. Kyra is on her way as well." The smell of hot pizza and garlic filled the space. Betha knew she needed to shower first. Otherwise, she was going to eat and then pass out filthy.

"Can we not?" asked Angie. "Can this just be food, family, and friends celebrating? We just did the impossible, and one night is not much to ask."

Grandpappy blinked, and Betha could feel how tired Angie was across the bond. It was the same for Carter and herself. This whole thing had been hard, and somehow, they had done it. A night off was important. Though her family wasn't quite complete yet. Eric was missing. Betha reached out to the bond in the back of her mind and felt him very close.

"We can wait, bunny," said Grandpappy. "It's been awhile since I had an adventure like that."

Another knock came and then the door opened to Eric peeking his head in. "Thank the fates." He walked in, and right on his heels was Susan. Maybe they had gotten up to some adventures as well. Betha blushed at the thought and forced her thoughts away from Eric's love life. He gave her a glance, and she just shook her head.

"You guys are back," continued Eric. Carter smiled at

his brother and gave him a tight hug. The two stayed connected for a moment before Carter pulled away. "It is so good to see you. How's your head?"

Carter chuckled. "Still hard as rock. I'm fine—you can stop worrying."

Betha climbed back to her feet and gave Eric a hug. Hopefully he didn't care that she was still a hot mess. "I think we decided tonight is family, food, and relaxing. No hard discussions." Eric opened his mouth, but then closed it and nodded.

Susan moved toward the pile of weapons in the corner. "Where did this come from?" she asked, holding the sword that Angie had brought back.

Betha shrugged and moved toward the hallway to take her turn in the shower. Angie answered Susan, but Betha ignored the conversation as she left the room. It could wait until tomorrow. Carter let her pass, then followed her down the space and into the bathroom. He closed the door softly behind him. The bathroom was giant. It had a soaker tub and a large walk-in shower with several shower heads. The tile was a bright white everywhere. Several different options for body wash and shampoo lined the shelving over the toilet.

"How are you doing?" he asked.

Betha gave him a very small smile. His hair was still wet, and strands dangled in his face. It took a moment, but she realized he looked younger than when he had been human. Her exhausted mind pushed those thoughts into a box. Wondering about the impacts of angelic manifestation on her boyfriend would definitely have to wait. "I'm right where all of us are. Tired. Ready for an epic shower, some food, then a nap. Well, sleep. I want at least eight hours of deep sleep with a comfy bed and blankets."

Carter smiled at her and nodded. "Let me grab you some sweats from the hall closet. Kyra has plenty in a variety of sizes for unexpected visitors."

She still had her armor on, since the concern was real that her clothes might fall apart as soon as she took it off. Next time she went on a multiple-world adventure, she would bring more changes of clothing. Then again, anything else added to her pack would probably make her scream. It had been heavy enough. The hot springs from Mountain Hold had been so long ago, which was the last time she had washed her clothes.

Carter set the clothes on the toilet and then gave her a hand with the armor. Betha turned around and faced the shower. "I'll add this to the pile. Tomorrow, that will be my job—making sure our gear is good." She held her arms up in the air, and he quickly unclipped everything. The boots were already off and back in the living room.

"We actually did it," said Betha. She stretched upward, then continued, "I knew we would, but at times I didn't know how."

"It all worked out, and you didn't leave me behind," he said from behind her. Then all of the armor was off, and she had only her ragged clothing. It all was going to get tossed, from her T-shirt to her socks.

"I wouldn't leave you behind. At least not intentionally."

He stepped closer to her, and she turned to face him. His finger touched the side of her face. His blue eyes stared down at her softly before he leaned forward and kissed her. Betha leaned into the kiss, and her hands trailed up his sides to his back. This was something she needed. Finally, she pulled back.

"I need to shower, and then food."

He gave her a goofy smile and nodded. He paused at the door and just stared for a moment. "Enjoy the hot water." Carter headed out of the bathroom and gave her privacy to finish getting undressed. She appreciated his gallantry, but also wished, just a little, that maybe he hadn't been quite such the gentleman. Then again, she really was filthy. And tired.

The hot water was so relaxing, and she tried to ignore the nearly black water running down the drain at the start. As she let the steam and water run over her, it slowly cleared, and as her muscles really started to relax, she reached for the body wash.

Betha didn't know what was next besides pizza and family. Being back on Terra felt strange. Angie was here, along with Carter and Eric, but she could feel the pulls on all of them. Something was on that dead world that called to Angie, and Carter wanted to help the trolls. Eric had something going on with Susan, not to mention whatever was happening with the angels. She knew none of those were her path, though she didn't know quite what her path was yet. But she knew Carter would be part of it.

That look on his face when he'd just stared at her came back. Had he been glowing?

~

THE NEXUS WAS EMPTY. Guards were posted outside the doors, but no one was inside. The Fey Wilds were secure. Nothing was traveling the treaty ways right now. Who knew what mood the fey lord was in. Much had happened, but Kyra could only think about what was coming. And the mistakes of her past.

Kyra had felt the pull toward the portal and left James with Anige and Betha. The path from the apartments to the Nexus was short. The pull increased as she walked down the hall and into the open space. One portal glowed bright white, almost silver. The one that she had kept closed, that no one had used for centuries. The feeling of her grandmother came from the other side of it. The portal pulsed and she stepped forward.

It was a message from the Anchor of a node. The first one she had received. Nodes could pass messages to various portals, and the Traveler it was meant for would feel the call. Nothing had come in the time she had been on Terra, but she had wanted it that way back then. The anger of the young adult she had been had faded decades ago. Now her heart ached as she realized that leaving home had been irrational. When Andrea's betrayal had come to light, she couldn't help but wonder how many years she had missed with her family.

Kyra's fingers brushed the surface of the portal, and her grandmother's voice rang out. "Move quickly, my granddaughter. I have sent word to other nodes of Andrea's actions, and her connections with the Seen. Other Travelers might come. Will come."

Kyra's hands shook. When she had come home, she'd known she'd need to anchor the Nexus if she wanted it to keep standing. She was on a timeline to do so. Tears came to her eyes, and she let herself crumble forward, arms wrapped around her middle. Everything was tangled up in this space. All of her emotions, all of her work for the past two centuries. Her love, her pain, her heartbreak, and her Anchors were in the middle of all of it. And now she had to resolve it all, quickly.

"Shh, it's okay dearie," whispered the small creature that had appeared beside her. The brownie's voice was soothing. Fuen had wandered through the elven portal after she had anchored it, then never left. She kept the Nexus, along with Kyra's apartments, clean. One of the bedrooms was hers. "You can do whatever you need to. You are stronger than you know." Her tiny hand rested on Kyra's arm.

"Oh, Fuen. I screwed up so horribly." Kyra wiped at the tears rolling down her face. "I need to fix it."

"Then you will. You are a fighter."

"I have to contact my Anchors."

The brownie flinched. "I'm so sorry, dearie." She patted Kyra's arm again. It all came back to her Anchors. They had helped cement the Accords by creating bonds with her and in turn with their people. Fuen knew of them, being as she was one. Kyra's Anchors were scattered, and not all sane. Unfortunately, she had learned the hard lesson of bonding with the wrong people. And now she needed to face it. Face them.

And it was going to be the hardest thing she had ever done.

DID YOU MISS TRAVELER FORGOTTEN? It's the story of the summer before Betha starts at St. Luna's! Sign up on my email list to get your copy!

~

WHILE YOU WAIT for the next Traveler book, return to the Nexus Universe in Visions of Blood and Feathers! Discover what some beloved side characters, including Eric and Susan, have been up to. Read Visions of Blood and Feathers now!

MEOW: MAGICAL EMPORIUM OF WARES

T ucked away on a quiet street, the bookstore doesn't have an address - but it doesn't need one, as it magically appears to those who are meant to find it.

THE JOB AD SEEMED AMAZING. I get to take care of this really neat bookstores that has an amazing espresso machine. There is this cute little black cat that sits on the counter and I get to live upstairs. What better opportunity could ever be out there, as I pay off my ungodly student loans?

Little did I know as soon as the paperwork was signed, I'd find out the cat talks, and magic might just be real? *Read on...*

TONI'S NOTES

Somehow, we are back on Terra. Heading to Sky World and saving the Gargoyles kicked a hornets nest that has drastic changes on other worlds. Not to mention, Betha is learning to stand on her own. Before we can dive back into Betha's story, there are some unanswered questions about what has been happening on Terra since she left.

We finally get to talk about some of those events in The Seer's Fate Series. As you can guess, the star of the show is going to be Susan... or is that who she really is? I'm super excited to finally get a chance to explore this character. I hope you are just as excited as I am!

While you wait for the next book, check out MEOW. It's a free serial that I post once a week. It's a cozy story that's slice of life, with magical moments. You have a magical bookshop, a talking cat, and now Sable the new shopkeeper who has to figure it all out!

To stay up to date join my newsletter: tonibinns.com

For book snippets, quotes and artwork check out my Instagram: @tonibinnsauthor